PRAISE FOR *BERTRAND COURT*

"With insight and empathy, Michelle Brafman portrays a wide range of interconnected characters who share heartbreak, indiscretions, and tantalizing secrets in this keenly observed multi-generational chronicle."

— J. Ryan Stradal, author of
Kitchens of the Great Midwest

"Michelle Brafman's gorgeous linked narratives focus on a group of astonishing characters, all grappling with power, lust, love, sex, and how best to be alive in a complicated world, all set against the backdrop of a Washington D.C. suburb. Gloriously alive, moving, and blazingly honest—*Bertrand Court* is brilliant."

— Caroline Leavitt, author of
Is This Tomorrow and *Pictures of You*

"Brafman eavesdrops on the human heart and reports back to us in *Bertrand Court* with honesty, compassion, and soul. This is gorgeous writing, in stories lit with grace."

— Dylan Landis, author of *Rainey Royal*

"In *Bertrand Court*, Brafman invites us to 'the family dinner table of life.' This is a beguiling collection of gently intertwining stories, celebrating in pellucid prose the infinite variations of 'normal.'"

— Mary Morrissy, author of *Prosperity Drive*

"I was in love with this novel-in-stories by page ten, and I stayed in love to the end. What a moving, powerful collection! It's like listening to the world's best gossip—someone who's happy to fill in her friends on the juicy details of their neighborhood, but does it with so little judgment and so much knowing and empathy that it makes you feel like a better, kinder citizen of the world. Read it—you'll feel loved, seen, and understood by this wonderful writer."

— REBECCA BARRY, author of
Later, at the Bar: A Novel in Stories

"Like a Jewish Anne Lamott, Brafman reels you in with warmth, depth, and heart."

— SUSAN COLL, author of *The Stager* and
events & programs director at Politics & Prose

PRAISE FOR *WASHING THE DEAD*

"A fast-paced and compelling debut."

— *Library Journal*

"Brafman examines the inner lives of her characters with the dexterity of a surgeon and the compassion of a saint."

— *Lilith Magazine*

"Heartfelt and genuine, *Washing the Dead* never betrays the complicated truths of family and tradition."

— DAVID BEZMOZGIS, author of *The Betrayers*

"Intimate, big-hearted, compassionate, and clear-eyed, Michelle Brafman's novel turns secrets into truths and the truth into the heart of fiction."

— AMY BLOOM, author of *Lucky Us*

"Compelling."

— *The New York Jewish Week*

"[A] striking debut novel."

— *The Jewish News Weekly*

"A heartfelt story of loss, hope, and reconciliation...[it] captures the complex essence of the mother-daughter relationship with honesty and sincerity."

— *Booklist*

"Brafman's astonishing compassion for all human frailty infuses this story about the need for truth and the promise of forgiveness."

— HELEN SIMONSON, author of *Major Pettigrew's Last Stand*

"[*Washing the Dead*] succeeds in showing how family history has a way of sneaking up on us from the depths of the past, shaping the present in ways both familiar and unexpected."

— *Haaretz*

"A rich tale of love, friendship, yearning, and forgiveness."

— JESSICA ANYA BLAU, author of *The Wonder Bread Summer*

Also by Michelle Brafman

Washing the Dead

BERTRAND COURT

Michelle Brafman

PROSPECT
·PARK·
BOOKS

Published by Prospect Park Books
2359 Lincoln Avenue
Altadena, CA 91001
www.prospectparkbooks.com

Distributed by Consortium Book Sales & Distribution
www.cbsd.com

Library of Congress Cataloging-in-Publication Data
Names: Brafman, Michelle, author.
Title: Bertrand court / Michelle Brafman.
Prospect Park Books, [2016]
Identifiers: LCCN 2016002128| ISBN 9781938849794 (hardback) |
ISBN 9781938849800 (paperback) | ISBN 9781938849817 (e-book)
Subjects: | BISAC: FICTION / Literary. | FICTION / Family Life. |
FICTION / Jewish.
Classification: LCC PS3602.R344415 B47 2016 | DDC 813/.6--dc23
LC record available at http://lccn.loc.gov/2016002128

Cover design by David Ter-Avanesyan.
Book layout and design by Amy Inouye, Future Studio.
Printed in the United States of America.

For Tom

The Solonsky Family & Forebears

Hannah, Eric, and Amy Solonsky — the Solonsky siblings
Simon Solonsky — their father
Goldie Solonsky — their grandmother and Simon's father
Sylvia Seigel — their great-aunt and Goldie's sister

Hannah's Family

Danny Weiss — Hannah's husband
Goldie, Jane, and baby number 5 — Hannah and Danny's children
Robin Weiss-Gold — Danny's sister
Marcus Gold — Robin's husband
Justin and Sydney — Robin and Marcus's children
Rosie Gold — Marcus's sister

Eric's Family

Maggie Stramm Solonsky — Eric's wife
Alec and Kaya — Eric and Maggie's children
Helene Stramm — Maggie's mother

Amy's Family

Leon Falk — Amy's husband

Related Characters

Becca Coopersmith — Hannah's college roommate
Adam Kornfeld — Becca's husband
Jason and Isaac — Becca and Adam's children
Georgia Dumfries — Former lover of Adam
Nikki Chamberlain — Georgia's best friend
Tad Chamberlain — Nikki's husband
Phil Scott — Eric Solonksy's partner/cameraman and former
    lover of Amy and Georgia
Molly Flanders — Phil's wife

Residents of Bertrand Court

Eric and Maggie Solonsky (and children)
Robin and Marcus Gold (and children)
Phil Scott and Molly Flanders
Becca Coopersmith and Adam Kornfeld (and children)

CONTENTS

SHHH

Baby #5 and Danny Weiss, March 1993

Y ou swim inside your mother's womb, and the sound of her heartbeat lulls you to sleep, and you wait for Michael, the archangel who spoke to Adam after Eve bit from the apple, and to Moses through the burning bush. Now he speaks to you. He teaches you everything, the languages of the pelicans and dolphins and tigers and the names of the eighty-eight constellations. He tells you secrets. Your father Danny's secrets, like stealing *Playboy* from his bar mitzvah tutor's briefcase, and your mother Hannah's secrets, like stealing Aunt Sylvia's spoon. You learn the names your parents give each other when they fight and when they love, and the names they gave to the babies that preceded you, Ruth, Zeke, Jacob, and Sylvia, the two who never made it past the first trimester and the two who did.

You know that the Jewish folktale about Michael is true, that he will speak to you for the last time seconds before you see your first glimpse of fluorescent hospital light. "Shhh," he'll whisper, pressing his cool, dry index finger into the island between the base of your nose and your upper lip, forming a valley dividing two tiny mountains of raised skin. And all that knowledge? Gone. You'll have to relearn everything. But while you're still inside the belly, you're smarter than Aristotle or Einstein or Voltaire or certainly your parents, who in an effort to birth you are behaving badly right now.

———

Danny pretends to read an article about the Cardinals' new pitcher, but he's really watching Hannah concentrate on a spinning bowl of egg whites, as if she could will them to peak. The steady rhythm of the electric beater makes him want to take a nap; everything makes him want to take a nap these days.

"My sister's not going to care if the cake doesn't have the meringue thing on top, sweetie," he offers, fairly confident that his attempt to simplify life for his wife will only annoy her.

"You told Robin?" Hannah turns to him, narrowing her eyes, which are round and almost black.

"Of course I didn't."

He wouldn't dare. The first time a second stripe materialized on the home pregnancy test they practically sent *The Washington Post* a press release announcing the news of their good fortune. This time, they shroud the pregnancy in secrecy because that's what Hannah wants; Danny doesn't know what he wants, or whether it's okay for him to want anything at all.

"Better not have." Hannah empties a bowl of limp egg whites into the trash, yet another failed attempt to bake this cake for her sister-in-law's belated birthday dinner. Robin is due at five with her husband, Marcus, and their two children, three-year-old Justin and infant Sydney.

Last week Hannah stir-fried chicken for her sister, Amy, on the verge of pummeling another poor guy's heart, and her brother, Eric, newly in love with a good-looking woman named Maggie, who seemed a little out of his league. But hosting Robin's family? Bad idea. Hannah's so jealous she can't even bring herself to touch the baby; she insists that they need to be around babies, however, because they avoided them during the last four pregnancies and see what happened? Danny's happiness for his sister feels like a betrayal to his wife.

The thermometer outside their kitchen window reads sixty-four degrees, balmy for a March day in Washington. Normally, they would take a walk along the canal through their Georgetown neighborhood, which would be teeming with students and suburban refugees lapping up "God's little hot flash" (his mother-in-law's term for this kind of weather). Blue skies would do them a world of good.

Hannah wipes a puddle of egg yolk off the counter, spraying the residue with a lemony-piney-smelling cleaner. "We need more eggs."

Danny sees this as an opening, and he folds up his paper. "Why don't we take a walk down M Street and scare up a cake?" His tone is tentative and too cheery at the same time. "I'll spring for a mocha."

"No caffeine or chocolate." She sighs. "Especially in the first trimester."

"How about citrus? I'll buy you an orange juice. Fresh squeezed." He feels like someone is sucking the energy from his body with a hose; if he doesn't leave the house now, he will lose his will to do so, maybe forever.

She rubs her neck, long and elegant like the rest of her body, and gives him a patronizing smile that screams, *The health of our baby rests on my baking this cake, but you, Mr. Lunkhead, would never get that.*

He gets more than she thinks. He's never mentioned the credit card statement revealing the handmade fertility drum she bought at an import store in Dupont Circle, or the visits to the psychic (it had never occurred to him that psychics accept Visa). And then there was the plane ticket to Milwaukee — $878 after she'd talked the airline into giving her a bereavement fare — to visit her barren aunt's grave. Don't ask because she won't tell you why.

"Come on, Hannah." He wants to yank her, actually both of them, from their row-house apartment, as if it were filling with smoke and fire.

"Can't you walk a few blocks alone?"

"Fresh air is good for the spirit." He's almost begging now. Pathetic.

The phone rings. "I bet it's your sister."

Hannah is right. It is Robin, who never begins a phone conversation with him by saying hello. "Justin and Marcus picked up some disgusting stomach bug. They've been getting sick all morning. I hope you guys haven't gone to the grocery store already."

"Don't worry about that. Just get everyone well." He can hear Sydney cooing in the background. "At least the baby didn't get it."

"Rain check?"

"Of course." Danny hangs up. "Snow day," he tells Hannah,

but she doesn't laugh at their code phrase for when fate allows them to skirt a social obligation.

"Whatever." She tosses the empty carton of eggs into the trash and doesn't mention the three grocery stores they've visited to shop for this dinner.

"At least we don't have to go back to the market now."

Hannah runs her hand through her bangs in that way she does when she's agitated. "Then can you just go and get a carton of milk or the Sunday *Times* or a new pair of boxers or...."

Her tone incites in him the smallest hit of adrenaline, just enough to hoist himself out of his chair. "I get it."

"Finally." She cracks one of her last eggs.

He grabs his car keys and the fleece jacket she gave him for his thirtieth birthday, four years ago, the night they first decided to make a baby. Their bellies full of steak and birthday sundaes, they made love and then fake-bickered over baby names. Christ, the hubris.

———

You'd think with all your learning you could find a way to break out of this uterus and tell your parents to relax. You want to congratulate your father for finally mustering himself to take a break from trying to cheer your mother up. You wish you could tell Hannah that she doesn't have to bake Grandma Goldie's icebox cake (the psychic instructed her to "connect" with her dead relatives) or spend a fortune on hucksters (although some are the real thing, like the palm reader who told her that she will have two healthy girls) or obsess that she's going to end up like her infertile dead aunt Sylvia, who contrary to family lore wasn't infertile at all. She would have had children if her husband hadn't insisted that they give up after a couple of miscarriages. Did you hear that, Hannah? She quit. She would have succeeded on the next try. Hang on.

———

Danny drives down M Street. Sunshine splashes the faces of college kids looping their elbows through the handles of Abercrombie & Fitch bags, sporting expensive eyewear, and laughing into the wind. "Enjoy it while it lasts," he mutters to them as he turns onto Wisconsin Avenue, cranking the volume on a Phish CD; Hannah detests jam bands, "the sophomoric lyrics and interminable guitar solos." She has a point; you have to be in the right mood, which he is.

Three lone cars occupy the Bethesda Bowl parking lot. It takes Danny's eyes a minute to adjust from the bright daylight to the dark bowling alley, whose familiar smell of stale beer and feet comforts him. The sporadic clunk of a solitary bowling ball hitting wood replaces the usual hum of laughter and cheering. He rents a pair of size elevens and picks out a thirteen-pound ball; he hasn't bowled without his own ball in years, and he's never had practically the whole alley to himself.

He keys his name into the electronic scoreboard and then on impulse types in Hannah's name too. He grabs a nine-pound ball and designates it as hers. When it's his turn, he bowls like Hannah, lugging the ball to the starting stripe, swinging his arm back spastically, heaving the ball down the alley and into the gutter. When it's Hannah's turn, he bowls like the St. Louis, Missouri, champ that he was, back when

Wednesday afternoons meant bowling with Russ Newman for a few hours after school. Afterward, they'd split a roast beef sub, the mayo and peppered vinegar drenching their swollen fingers, and dream up schemes to audition for *Bowling for Dollars*. By the time they figured out they'd been watching reruns, they'd gone on to different high schools.

The next game, he picks up Hannah's ball but releases it, feeling its weight curl down his palm to his fingertips and into the ball return rack. The hell with Hannah Solonsky. He plays both turns like himself. Strike. Strike. Strike. He's as juiced up as he was the night he won the Spare No Strike Bowling Alley's thirteen-and-under title. The sound of the pins crashing into each other makes his heart pump faster. Maybe they installed microphones at the end of the lanes to rev up the players.

He figures a beer would go down nicely right now. Sitting in a dark, overheated bowling alley and downing a Heineken on a warm, sunny afternoon feels decadent as hell. No Hannah. He can breathe.

As he's settling with the bartender for his second beer, he catches sight of a couple standing by the cigarette machine dry-humping each other like teenagers. But they're not. Strands of gray streak the woman's dark hair, and she's wearing low-cut jeans that are doing some very nice things for her ass; the man is practically twice her height and balding.

Danny and Hannah used to be like that. One time they did it in the laundry room of the Hotel Washington, on Hannah's dare, at Danny's company Christmas party, right after his boss announced that he'd made Rookie Realtor of the Year. And to think they'd worried about using birth control. What a joke.

The couple must feel Danny staring at them, because they both look up. Oh, man, it's Sam, his new client, with a woman who is not his wife. Sam looks at Danny like he's just been busted shoplifting porn from a 7-Eleven.

Danny walks over to Sam and the woman who is not Sam's wife and blurts out, "My wife's pregnant. Don't tell anyone."

Sam pauses, looking at Danny as though he's not sure he heard him correctly. "Congratulations." He gives Danny a half smile.

Danny's tired of Hannah shushing him. Giving this pregnancy some air feels pretty damn great, like those first few steps you walk at the end of a jog. And who better to entrust with this secret than a husband who's just been caught sticking his tongue down another woman's throat? And then Danny does something that would evoke a week of Hannah's scorn: He points at the woman and gives Sam the thumbs-up sign. And he means it. Here's to spontaneous sex. He brings the ice-cold beer bottle to his lips. *L'chaim.*

––––––

You want to tell your father that he's not the only one hiding in the dark on a beautiful day, that Hannah is sitting alone in a matinee, eating buttered popcorn and sipping Sprite. You want to tell your parents so many things, like "Stop eating that popcorn, Hannah; you're going to have heartburn later." Or "She doesn't mean to be such a shrew, Danny, it's the fear and the hormones talking." You want to shout in your father's ear, "Remember when you tried to impress Hannah by letting her drag you on a rafting trip down the Colorado River and you were so scared that the only thing that kept you from fainting was watching her muscles contract with each paddle stroke and listening to her laugh?" You want to yell, "Smoother waters ahead. Don't panic. You'll drown!"

———

Danny's approaching Westmoreland Circle when he notices that he forgot to change out of his bowling shoes. He's careening out of control, like a balloon that escapes when you're blowing it up. He returns his shoes to the bowling alley and makes up an excuse to visit his big sister by stopping at Barnes and Noble to buy her a birthday present, an Indigo Girls live CD. Robin loves chick music.

He turns onto Robin's street, Bertrand Court, and sits in his car for a few minutes before he cuts off the engine. Out of habit, he surveys the houses. The cul-de-sac reminds him of the one where he and his sisters grew up, and he finds comfort in the tire swings hanging from oak trees, the creaky gliders nestled on big front porches, the basketball hoops planted on garages filled with cars designed to haul around lots of kids. Most of the houses are Dutch Colonials and American Foursquares — about twenty-five hundred square feet — save for the old Victorian on the corner, the show house with the bad feng shui. Two of Robin's neighbors have placed brightly colored Adirondack chairs on their front lawns. If he ever sells a house on this block, he'll buy the new owners one of those chairs. It's the kind of touch that generates referrals.

Danny's saving to buy a house for his own family, even though Hannah won't move to the suburbs right now. She claims she'll feel more pressured to fill up the rooms of a big suburban spread. She doesn't buy into Danny's "If you build it, they will come" motto (she won't even watch *Field of Dreams* with him anymore, though she's always had a thing for Kevin Costner). She used to think Danny's baseball fixation was cute, along with his perfect attendance record at his Young Judea summer camp reunions and his knowledge of the hand motions to the song "David Melech Yisrael." She told him that he made her feel safe, but not just teddy-bear safe. Big, beefy orgasm safe, too. Or so she said. Either way, he sure doesn't know how to make her feel safe anymore.

As he walks toward the house, he hears laughter coming from the backyard. It's Justin and Marcus. Does the stomach flu make people laugh? He walks around back, and Justin is sitting cross-legged on their new trampoline, while Marcus, still built like a former high school wrestling champion, gently jumps up and down, bouncing his son's skinny little body. They both look perfectly healthy.

Robin emerges from the back door, toting Sydney in one of those front-loading baby-carrier contraptions. "Wash up, guys. The lasagna's getting cold."

"Didn't Mom used to make us toast when we had the stomach flu?" Danny asks his sister, in the same tone he used in their youth to bust both of his older sisters for their curfew infractions.

Robin, startled, gives Danny a look as sheepish as the one Sam gave him at the bowling alley half an hour earlier.

He pictures Hannah cracking egg after egg trying to bake that cake for his sister, and he thinks he should feel angry or betrayed. But he doesn't. "So, did you put turkey sausage in the lasagna this time?" Within seconds, he's swept up into the business of dinnertime. The kitchen smells of garlic and the red wine that Robin has opened for Marcus, who is madly in love with her, and is the kind of guy who'd leave a twenty-five-percent tip on a bad meal. His sister scored big. Danny aches for her kitchen: the fridge adorned with a list of emergency phone numbers and a Thomas the Tank Engine birthday party invitation for Justin, the high chair propped against the window, the four pink pacifiers drying on a paper towel.

"I'll hold Sydney; you guys eat." He nods to Robin and Marcus. Sydney, all cartilage and baby skin, feels lighter than a bag of groceries. She's almost four months old, but she still smells shrink-wrap new. Her mouth is shaped like the base of a pear; her skin is dark, like her father's; and her eyes are turning brown, like his own eyes, the Weiss eyes, the color of fresh mud. This is the first time he's really looked into his niece's eyes. Will his baby inherit them, too? He's never held her so close to his body that he could feel her warm, shallow breaths through his T-shirt. How could he have? Not with Hannah wincing every time he reached for Sydney. His body relaxes into his longing, and for a moment, the emotional riptide that pulls him between Robin and Hannah relents into a soft wave.

When Sydney starts to cry, Robin attaches her to her breast with one arm and shovels forkfuls of lasagna into her mouth with the other. Strands of hair, pumpkin- colored like his and Justin's, have escaped from her ponytail, and her cheekbones hide under an added layer of flesh.

Danny's starving. He butters a slice of day-old bread from

Marcus's bakery and fills half a dinner plate with lasagna. Cheese, noodles, and warm bread. Comfort food. He doesn't want to leave his sister's kitchen. Not now. Not ever.

Justin kneels next to Danny's chair with a worn copy of *The Very Hungry Caterpillar*, and Danny pulls the little guy onto his lap and reads. Marcus gives him the bedtime signal. After Justin climbs off Danny's lap, he turns around and grins. A simple gesture that makes Danny's heart feel like it will explode through his ribs. The ache returns. The ache that makes him want to nap and stay late at the office, feigning paperwork.

Danny clears the plates while Sydney dozes off in her baby seat and Robin loads the dishwasher. He feels his sister watching him eye a bakery box of half-eaten birthday cake, a sheet cake decorated with pink flowers and the last two letters of "Mommy" written in red frosting.

"I almost forgot." Danny retrieves the CD from his jacket pocket and hands it to Robin.

"Oh, Danny." She wipes her hands on her jeans and takes the gift, shaking her head in embarrassment. "Sydney and I don't bring out the best in Hannah these days."

"It's okay." And it is.

"No, it's not. That was shitty of me to lie about being sick."

He interrupts her mid-apology. "Hannah's pregnant again." This is his second rebellion against her gag order. "I'm not supposed to tell anyone yet."

"Can I give you a hug?" Robin's eyes are filling with tears.

Danny does not feel like a person who has just delivered good news. He betrayed Hannah's secret to Sam because he felt like his back might break from its weight; he betrayed her secret to his sister because he wants someone to call if it doesn't work out, and kind, level-headed Robin would be his first choice. Just because he can't bleed or cramp, or stick hormone shots into his thigh, that doesn't mean this doesn't hurt like hell, doesn't mean he can do this alone. Goddammit, he wants someone to prop him up, to tell him that everything's going to be all right. Does that make him a jerk?

"I better get home." He kisses his sister's cheek. "Good lasagna."

Robin crosses two fingers for good luck and kisses them.

When Danny slips into bed next to Hannah that night, she rolls her back into his chest and he buries his face in her hair. Words mean nothing now. Instead of offering her a pep talk about the pregnancy, he listens to the rhythm of her breaths, wrapping one arm under her ribs and pulling her into his body until they are one. They breathe in synchrony, and for the first time in months he feels a slender wedge between himself and her fear. Between himself and the insidious sense of doom that accompanied the second stripe on their last test stick.

When he wakes up in the middle of the night to go to the bathroom, he finds Hannah's side of the bed empty. He stumbles into the kitchen, still warm from her baking. The counters shine, the sink sparkles, and the scent of Comet and chocolate and sugar envelops him. Against the back door she's propped a plastic trash bag bursting with empty egg cartons and cracked shells, yolks sticking to the side of the bag.

The house is so still that he can detect a slight rustle coming from the den. Hannah sits spine straight on the only hard chair in the room; the weak light from the lamp forms a nimbus around her hair. She's so pretty. One hand rests on a pressed white linen napkin blanketing her belly, and the other slides a forkful of perfect meringue icebox cake into her mouth.

———

You feel the warmth of Michael's angel breath in your ear, whispering something about stubborn morsels of knowledge. Call them intuition, sixth sense, or gut feelings. He speaks in an unfamiliar voice, tender and barely audible, when he tells you that your parents' instincts are right. You're not going to make it. You'll never see that fluorescent hospital light. No nurse will slap your behind or swaddle you in a striped hospital blanket or cover your head with a beige cap tied with a baby blue ribbon.

Your mother will start bleeding eight days from now. Thirteen weeks. She'll get pregnant again next January, but she won't bond with your sister Goldie for a few months; she'll be too afraid that it's not for keeps. Slowly she'll return to normal. She'll welcome Jane into the world with less trepidation.

Time will pass, and they'll forget what a wreck Hannah was when she was carrying you. They'll forget about the deals she made with God and the tarot cards she hid in a Quaker Oats tin and the "I'm sorry"s and "I love you"s she muttered to dead relatives. You'll become a war story they'll swap with other couples who had trouble conceiving, but only the ones who finally give birth to healthy children.

Every few years, on your due date, your parents will wake

up at dawn and curl themselves around each other and for a fast second let themselves imagine that dinner will end with cupcakes and candles. Throughout the day, you'll tickle their memories as your father mows the lawn or your mother reads *Harold and the Purple Crayon* to Goldie and Jane. Sometimes, your absence will crash into their consciousness like a wreck on I-95. They'll attend a party for a child who shares your birthday, and they'll think that if you'd made it, it would be you tearing the wrapping paper from that Luke Skywalker action figure or giggling in the moon bounce or begging for a second piece of cake. To quiet these thoughts, they'll tell themselves, "But then, if that baby had made it, we wouldn't have had Goldie or Jane," and that strange logic will enable them to escort you back to your hiding place, in the crevices of their souls.

TWO TRUTHS AND A LIE
Amy Solonsky, June 2001

A my Solonsky didn't mind being the family fuckup. It took
the pressure off. Nobody expected her to turn up on
time for family events, and if she drank too much wine
or showed too much thigh or lit up a cigar with Uncle Herman
while the other women cleared the dishes, well, she gave her
relations a reason to revel in their own good manners.

Amy arrived at her sister Hannah's birthday potluck
empty-handed and two hours late. Hannah's college friend,
Becca Coopersmith, was hosting the party at her home on
Bertrand Court, or "White Picket Fenceville," as Amy had
nicknamed the suburban cul-de-sac located six or so miles
north of her D.C. apartment. She let herself in the back door.
The house was quiet, and the buffet of leafy green salads and
quinoa dishes had been picked over. A half-eaten chocolate
birthday cake sat on the counter.

Hannah was standing alone in Becca's kitchen opening
a bottle of Chardonnay. Amy couldn't get used to her sister's gauntness. A few months ago, without warning, they'd
lost their father, and Hannah had dropped ten pounds she

couldn't afford to lose.

"The ladies are out back." Hannah motioned with the corkscrew.

"Where are the kids?" Amy had been looking forward to seeing Goldie and Jane.

Hannah tapped her watch. "It's *slate*, Amy. Danny took them home."

"Hannah, are you *slurring*?" Amy said, popping an artisanal olive into her mouth.

"You calling me a shicker?" Hannah punched the first syllable of their father's Yiddish term for a drunk. She removed the cork and giggled.

"Oh my God, what have you done with my sister?" Hannah was the designated driver, always. Amy and their brother, Eric, called her the "perfect child."

"Beats me. I'm not even annoyed that you missed the kids." Hannah took a few wobbly steps toward Amy. She normally moved with the grace of an acrobat.

"Careful there, party girl."

Hannah, strong for such a sylphlike woman, embraced Amy so hard that she almost gasped.

"Happy birthday." Amy squeezed her back.

Hannah slid out of Amy's arms and picked up a plate loaded with frosting. "Here, I saved this for you."

Becca entered the kitchen with a handful of dirty forks. She tossed them into the sink and watched Amy scoop up a glob of icing with her finger and lick it.

"Amy, hi, and that's gross," Becca said.

"Not gross. Major deliciousness." Amy's siblings habitually

heaped their frosting on her plate while their mother looked on disapprovingly. Amy's excesses made her parents uncomfortable. To Amy's surprise, though, tonight the frosting tasted too buttery and left an oily residue on her tongue.

"Wash your hands, and I'll greet you properly." Becca pointed to the sink.

Amy rinsed her finger and then Becca hugged her.

"Why do you two smell like the inside of a bonfire?" Amy fanned her face.

"We've come here tonight to covet Becca's new fire pit," Hannah said. "And play some game."

They knew that Becca's real mission for the party was neither to show off the fire pit nor play a parlor game nor even celebrate Hannah's birthday, but to cheer up Hannah. She had been flying back to Milwaukee most weekends to help her mother sort and dispose of the remains of her dad's life. A few days after the funeral, Amy feebly volunteered to take a shift but never followed up on the offer.

"Come on, let's go outside." Hannah grabbed the bottle of wine and walked toward the back door.

"We're right behind you," Becca said, and then she turned to Amy and mouthed, "I'm worried about her."

"I know." Amy mouthed back, not sure of what else to say or how to comfort her sister either. Hannah was much better at this kind of thing. She'd offered the perfect words to every mourner who attended their father's shiva, but it was Amy who'd picked out the casket and propped up their mother while it was being lowered into the ground.

Becca scrutinized Amy. "You, on the other hand, are

glowing."

"I don't know about that, Bec, but thanks." Amy wrapped a long black curl around her finger. This morning her new boyfriend, Leon, had washed her hair with lemon-scented shampoo. He was an architect fifteen years her senior, and like Amy, who was a graphic designer, he thought in shapes and pictures. Leon was still a secret. If Hannah knew about him, she would theorize that Amy was dating an older man to replace her father. Amy had met Leon on the flight to Milwaukee for the funeral. Unlike her father, Leon worshipped her, and she found herself welcoming this new kind of love, which seemed to be changing her a little bit each day.

"Come covet my fire pit." Becca led Amy through the mudroom, cluttered with her sons' cleats and backpacks.

It was an unusually cool night for June, too cold for the lightning bugs. Amy hadn't thought to bring a sweater and shivered in her halter top and shorts. The sky was clear, but the air rippled with smoke. Becca walked past her prized hydrangeas toward ribbons of orange flames contained in a knee-high circle of cement and exquisite stone.

"Ta-da!" she said, thrusting her arms up like Mary Lou Retton sticking a vault. "What do you think?"

The fire pit sat in the center of a carpet of pebbles. Hannah and two other women, swaddled in a rainbow assortment of Becca's Pashmina shawls, were settled into Adirondack chairs around the pit. Hannah was talking quietly with her sister-in-law Robin. On her other side sat Maggie, their brother Eric's wife. They all were drinking wine out of mason jars while their husbands were home getting the children ready for bed.

Becca leaned down and picked up a pebble. "Adam collected many of these from the Dead Sea."

"Very nice," Amy said neutrally, trying not to invite Becca to opine about West Bank settlements or related topics, or really any topic. The sooner they played the game, the sooner she could go home, or to Leon's. She'd told him that she was going to sleep in her own bed tonight, but now she didn't want to, and she didn't have to. He'd just given her a key to his house, a grown-up abode a few 'burbs over, with a garage and a washer and dryer.

"Come sit." Robin patted the chair next to her with her delicate hygienist's hand. Robin was her favorite member of the Bertrand Court posse. Amy didn't have dental insurance, and every six months, Robin cleaned her teeth for free after her boss left for the evening.

Amy wrapped herself in the soft red shawl Becca handed her, sat down, and hugged her knees to her chest, her silver rings, one on each stubby finger, glinting in the firelight.

Hannah thrust a bottle of tequila across Maggie's chair toward Amy. "Look, it's even got the worm. Becca bought it just for you."

Amy accepted the bottle and put it on the ground. "No thanks."

"What's got into you? Our Amy would put a dent in the bottle," Becca said.

"And get so snockered that I'd have to drive her home, but first . . ." Hannah waved her index finger in the air. "She'd make me drop her off at a hipster bar to meet up with her hipster friends."

"Maybe I'm not the Amy you know," Amy said quietly.

"Since when?" Hannah demanded.

"Since I'm the one driving your drunk butt home tonight." Maggie and Robin lived on Bertrand Court, but Hannah lived one suburb over.

"Well okay, then." Robin changed the subject. "What's this game of yours, Bec?"

"It's called Two Truths and a Lie. You have to tell three things about yourself, and two of them have to be true, but one is a lie, and we have to guess which."

"We play this at our retreats all the time." Maggie squared her shoulders, channelling her diversity-trainer affectation. "It's a highly effective way to force a vulnerability that creates community."

Amy reminded herself that Maggie only acted like an ass when she was nervous, her episodic sanctimoniousness making her an easy mark for the family gossipers. It didn't help that she was abnormally pretty.

"How true do these truths have to be?" Robin asked. "True true or embarrassing true?"

Amy wanted out of this forced fun. The light from the flames flattered the women, who sat with their hands in their laps as if they were meditating or praying. They gazed into the fire, perhaps scouring their pasts for truths and lies. Dating Leon had made Amy realize that she was exhausted from the truths of her life. Exhausted from making booty calls to hot, noncommittal men and working sixty-hour weeks. Exhausted from the adrenaline highs that fueled her, followed by the crashes, during which she'd escape to Hannah's for a

warm meal and movie night with Goldie and Jane, whom she
adored. Hannah would send Amy home with Tupperware
containers of hearty stews. But now Leon cooked for Amy,
and last Sunday, after a long morning in bed, she made him a
quiche. She burned the frozen crust she'd bought at the Safe-
way, but it was a start.

"Okay, you begin, Becca." Hannah took an enormous swig
of wine straight from the bottle. "This is your show."

"Well, all right." Becca stood and placed her hands on her
ample hips. "Number one," she said, snapping the waistband
of her flowing skirt, "I go commando every day.

"Number two, I got poison ivy in my hoo-ha after eating
shrooms and galloping around naked in the woods at the
summer camp where Adam and I met."

"Honey, you might regret this tomorrow," Robin said
gently.

Becca ignored Robin. "Three, I flushed Isaac's betta down
the toilet, but I think it was still alive."

Hannah blurted, "You do so wear panties, Becca. The
commando thing is the lie."

The women turned toward Hannah. Her elbow slipped off
the wide arm of the Adirondack chair, and she tried to relocate
it. "What? We do hot yoga together," she said, inciting a round
of laughter. "I've seen the panties. I've seen the hoo-ha too."

"I'm cutting you off." Amy reached for Hannah's bottle,
but her sister clutched it to her body. Amy was more startled
by Hannah's drunkenness than she was by Becca's statements
about her lower regions. Becca was a seeker, and over the years
she'd persuaded Hannah to study Kabbalah and irrigate her

colon, and she was already planning their fortieth-birthday trek to Nepal, even though the milestone was three years off.

"Your turn, Robin," Becca said.

Robin stood and unraveled herself from her Pashmina, a muted amber that matched her hair. "Past my bedtime."

"Wimp!" Hannah bellowed.

"I've got a patient coming in at seven tomorrow morning," Robin said.

Without Robin, Amy thought, things are going to get a little wild and mean. The scent of the smoke in the air was beginning to feel cloying.

"We'll fill you in on everyone's dirt." Hannah leaned back in her chair and held out her arms to Robin.

Robin kissed each of the women on the cheek and then walked over to Hannah, squatted down, and placed her palm on Hannah's cheek. "Happy birthday, sweetie." She turned to Amy. "Will you make sure she gets home?"

"Of course." The role of the responsible sibling felt like the puffy down coat her mother had bought her last year for Hanukkah —matronly, but deliciously warm on those cold January walks to the Metro.

"Your turn, Hannah," Becca said.

"I'm not ready." Hannah was watching the fire as if she couldn't tear her eyes away.

Becca pointed from Amy to Maggie until she stopped triumphantly at Maggie.

"No, I'm going last," Maggie said.

"All right, I'll go," Amy said. "Give me one second." She wanted a cigarette. She thought about revealing that since

her father died she couldn't shake the image of him standing behind her, guiding her through the motion of throwing
a baseball. The memory of his hand cupping hers barely
loosened the tight knot of tears that she would not, could not,
release.

Amy adjusted her glasses. Here's the truth she wanted to
say: Since their father's death, she awakened every day feeling freer than ever before. She looked directly at Hannah and
opened her mouth.

"I don't floss every day."

"Don't let Robin hear you say that, Amy," Maggie said.

"Not after all the free cleanings." Hannah chimed in.

Becca tapped Amy on the knee. "You can do better, Amy. I
told you about my hoo-ha."

Amy opened up her mouth to confess: She had a new
lover, and he was sweet and solid, and this monogamy thing
was kind of nice. Instead: "Two, in high school, I hid my weed
in the basement, in one of Hannah's ice skates."

Becca rose from her chair and picked up a poker from behind the pit. She stoked the fire until it spit out a fresh wave of
flames.

"I've known that for years, Amy," Hannah said. "You're giving us nothing. Nada."

The hell with them. She'll tell them about Leon. That
the sex was quiet but deeply satisfying. That they laughed
over nothing. "Three, I'm in love with a widower who owns a
WeedWacker."

"A widower who owns a WeedWacker! Sounds like the
punch line to a joke," Hannah said.

Amy glared at Hannah.

Hannah fake-glared back and imitated Amy folding her arms across her chest. "Prunella."

Prunella the witch. Amy cringed at the nickname their father used whenever she used to throw a tantrum or gave the stink eye to a relative she didn't like.

"The not flossing is the lie," Becca said. "Has to be."

"Amy never used to floss. It's the WeedWacker boyfriend," Hannah said.

"I floss plenty," Amy muttered.

Hannah nodded knowingly. "You'd eat WeedWacker man alive."

Eat him alive, Hannah? Nice. Real nice. The Solonskys made a sport out of teasing Amy, and she no longer wanted to serve as their chew toy. "Whatever."

Hannah cleared her throat loudly. She removed a rubber band from her wrist and put her hair in a messy bun. "I'm ready. Number one—"

Amy cut her off by clapping her hands. "Number one. Hannah ate a cherry tomato in the grocery store without paying for it." She laughed, but the sound that came out of her was sharply edged, not her bleat that everyone said was contagious. Hannah gave her sister one of her bemused smiles. "Are you done?" Okay, now they'd safely resumed their assigned places at the family dinner table of life.

"Not yet, angel." Amy reached into her bag and pulled out a pack of Marlboros. Nobody smoked in this zip code. Leon hated it when she lit up. She tweezed out a cigarette and tapped it against the arm of the chair. "Number two, Hannah

removed the tag from her new mattress." Amy noticed Becca
and Maggie looking at each other with "There she goes again"
expressions. Yeah, there she goes, right to the fire. Amy got
up and leaned into the pit, the heat fogging her glasses as she
brought her cigarette to the tip of a flame and breathed in.

"Jesus, Amy," Becca said. "You're going to burn your face
off."

Amy took a long drag. "That's Hannah. Boring, boring,
boring," she said as she exhaled, blowing smoke up toward the
moon.

"Okay, time to give your sister a turn, Amy," Becca said as
if she'd just settled a squabble over who got to ride shotgun in
the Solonsky family car. Hannah always rode in front despite
the fact that Eric was older and Amy was the only one in the
family with a sense of direction.

"You'll have to forgive Amy," Hannah said.

"Now, that's a line we've never heard before." Amy flicked
ash on the grass.

"Number one." Hannah put her bottle down on the grass.
"I gave my in-laws food poisoning the first time I cooked
Thanksgiving dinner."

Lie. Amy yawned. The dinner turned out perfectly, of
course. She was there.

"Number two, I had a crush on a Wiggle."

"Ew, she did. It was Murray." Amy took one last drag on her
cigarette and tossed the butt into the fire.

"Don't interrupt, Amy. That's cheating," Maggie said.

"Not like I was interrupted or anything," Amy muttered
under her breath.

"It's okay." Hannah sighed deeply. She shrugged off the Pashmina. She and Amy had inherited their mother's lovely collarbones, but now Hannah's protruded out of her body like wings.

Amy snorted. "Drum roll please."

"Number three." Hannah spoke so softly that the women leaned toward her.

"Number three, I stole a sterling silver baby spoon from my dead Aunt Sylvia."

Hannah's truth hung suspended in the air, like a wrecking ball in repose.

Amy was the first to speak. "What *spoon*? Why?"

"For another time, Amy." Hannah continued to stare into the fire, and Maggie and Becca glanced at each other but said nothing.

Only Amy looked at Hannah. "You robbed the dead?" she whispered.

Hannah rubbed her eyes with her fists, like a baby, and when she removed her hands, a mascara-stained tear ran down her left cheekbone.

"Holy shit, Hannah," Amy said.

"Yeah, holy shit," Hannah said.

Becca stood up. "Game's over, ladies."

Amy watched from her chair while Hannah and Maggie silently folded their shawls into neat squares, handed them back to Becca, and walked through the dewy grass to the kitchen and their sullied serving dishes. Amy had no platter to claim, so she stayed outside by the fire, wondering what the hell was happening to the Solonskys. Their mother, a stoic

German Jew, was weeping into Hannah's phone eight times a day, Eric the atheist had joined a synagogue where he said kaddish every morning before work, and Amy was burning quiches for a love interest. How well did Amy know her family? How well did she know herself? How well do you know anyone until you've seen them grieve?

The flames faded while the cicadas whined and an airplane passed over Bertrand Court. Amy eased herself out of her chair. A shovel lay behind the fire pit. She grabbed it, scooped up the embers, and spread the ashes evenly before she sprinkled them with the last few drops of Hannah's wine. It was time to take her sister home.

SYLVIA'S SPOON

Hannah Solonsky, June 1992

I steal a sterling silver baby spoon from my great-aunt Sylvia while her body, barely cold, rests under a blanket of disheveled earth at the Beth Shalom Cemetery. I do it in her kitchen, on impulse, while I'm looking for a teaspoon to stir my chamomile, seconds before my family begins reciting the mourner's kaddish in my aunt's living room. *Yisgadal ve yiskadash shema rabah, amen.*

My mother, loud and tone-deaf, can't even finish the prayer she's so weepy. We all are. She enters the kitchen to put a handful of used Kleenex into the trash, and I slide the spoon further into my pocket. I run my fingers around the tiny bowl and up along the skinny handle to the tip, which is inscribed with the Hebrew letter *hey*. My name, Hannah Solonsky, begins with a *hey*; this piece of flatware is my destiny. Besides, finders keepers.

I imagine that this spoon has survived pogroms and a long passage to Ellis Island, and I want to siphon its fortitude for my baby. I'm thirteen weeks pregnant, my new record for not miscarrying. Every morning I pray from *The Jewish Women's*

Guide to Fertility, a book I would have snickered at two years ago. I suffer the indignity of progesterone suppositories — the added hormones make me throw up in my office trash can — and I avoid foods I ate and clothes I wore while unsuccessfully carrying babies one through three. I take pregnancy yoga classes to manage the stress from keeping it all straight.

Danny can't win. If he's enthusiastic about the baby, I tell him not to jinx things. If he's cautious, I interrogate him — a man of reason, not instinct — about his "true gut" on this pregnancy. My parents are no help; my mother worries so much that I end up comforting her, and my father changes the subject but then emails me the cell phone numbers of his old med school buddies who specialize in fertility. My siblings have always leaned on me, and they wouldn't get it anyway. Eric is trying to mate, and Amy is consumed with being Amy. Most of my friends are reveling in their fecundity. I cling to this spoon and the hope that my dead aunt is taking care of my baby somewhere out there in the ether.

On the flight home from the funeral, I watch the Milwaukee homes, adorned with pink flamingos and aboveground swimming pools, disappear into a puff of clouds, and I sip lukewarm orange juice out of a plastic cup. I like the way my aunt's spoon rests against my thigh. Aunt Sylvia used to laugh at my knock-knock jokes and hang my art projects on her fridge and look the other way when I pinched pieces of meringue from the top of her icebox cake. I feel more hopeful than I have in weeks.

The plane is hovering over the Potomac when I kiss Danny's cheek, breathing in the familiar scent of Dial soap. "Let's name our baby Sylvia." As soon as these words leave my lips, I want them back.

Danny gives me the wan smile he's cultivated. "Let's just see what happens." He strokes my arm.

"Oh God, Danny. Don't tell me you're too superstitious to name the baby," I say, when in fact I cling to superstition like Velcro. I lean my head back and close my eyes, signaling that the conversation is over. My hand rests on my mildly distended belly as I daydream about my little Sylvia. It will be a warm spring day, and she'll sit on my lap licking vanilla icing off a cupcake, wiping her sticky fingers on my knees. She'll smell like baby sweat and sugar. I'll smooth her tangle of ringlets — auburn like Danny's — away from her eyes. I can practically hear her giggle. Fear forms in the back of my throat and swells into my esophagus like a hive, as it always does when I allow myself to hope that this baby will survive.

Later that night, shortly after eleven, I feel like someone is yanking my abdomen shut with a drawstring. Shit. Cramps turn into nausea, and I beg my baby to stay put. Danny pages the obstetrician while I stumble to the bathroom, clutching the spoon. Talisman in hand, I negotiate with God. No deal. Before the sun rises, I deliver my baby.

I rest my head against the side of the toilet and gaze at the emptied contents of my womb. I try to capture the clump of blood and tissue with my aunt's spoon, but my efforts only loosen it into a spray of red and greenish gray that dissolves into the bowl. I let my fingers linger in the cold red water before I close the lid. Aunt Sylvia appears to me: the slightly bulging gray eyes and the lisp and the sad smile pasted on soft, pink lips.

Danny mops my forehead with a washcloth. I stand up slowly and rinse off the spoon, turning the faucet on full blast in a futile attempt to drown out the sound of the flushing toilet.

One week later, Danny lounges on our bed staring slack-jawed at ESPN, as he has done for each of the past six nights. Who gives a damn about the Cardinals?

I forage in our pantry for Tylenol. We're out of cereal. A jar of homemade raspberry jam, our annual holiday gift from Robin, sits next to a bottle of capers; the colors remind me that I did get to see my actual baby, instead of just a black sonogram screen devoid of the pulsing light the size of a thumbtack. We disposed of those babies during tidy office visits followed by written instructions to call if there was too much blood. There's always too much blood.

I dump four tablespoons of jam and eight capers into a bowl and then retrieve the spoon from my purse; I use it to mix the concoction and ladle it into a small Ziploc baggie. Sylvia.

By the time I return to Danny, baggie and spoon in hand, he's asleep on our bed, his face bathed in the blue TV light, his mile-long eyelashes, blond at the tips, fanning the tender skin beneath his eyes. He looks like he's eleven years old. A fresh soul. The foot rubs and the phone calls from the office aren't working, but at least he's trying. I can't muster up the energy to comfort him. Before the miscarriages, I would have cheered him up by taking him bowling or seducing him or renting a Monty Python movie; we'd sit in front of the television drinking cheap beer and eating potato chips, laughing — Danny at John Cleese's ridiculousness, me at Danny — until we could barely breathe.

It's hot for June, and the breeze from the air-conditioning vent chills my toes. I turn off the light, pull my T-shirt over my head, and crawl into bed beside him, cradling his smooth back against my breasts. He mumbles something and reaches over to grab my hip. I move slightly, and he rolls over and runs his hands through my dirty hair. We don't make love — too raw, too soon. Sleep finds me still clutching the baggie of raspberry jam and capers and Aunt Sylvia's spoon.

The next morning, I cancel my nine o'clock staff meeting. I was scheduled to fly to Boston the day after I miscarried, so now the whole office knows what happened, compromising my status as den mother of our "little nonprofit that could." I'm going to have to face my coworkers. Best to get it over with, so at noon I stop by the office to pick up some files, and they treat me like I've got a raging case of pinkeye, except for Valerie, the stripper turned receptionist, who has a six-year-old son. She greets me with a homemade loaf of banana bread she's been keeping in her desk drawer for me. I almost cry.

I go home and try to nap. Nothing doing, so I pull on an old pair of shorts from my Bucky Badger days and walk two blocks up M Street to a coffeehouse that doesn't sell anything beginning with the letters "frap." Danny wants to move to Bethesda, but the thought of living in the suburbs without children thoroughly depresses me.

A cell-phone-blabbing mother spills her latte on me; the hot liquid burns my thigh. "Watch where you're going," she says, and her brusque words crack me open like a walnut. Instead of crying, I find a table and rub my iced tea against my leg.

A man with kind eyes and a thumb ring sits down next to me and asks to borrow a pen. I reach into my purse, and the baggie falls to the table. We both examine it.

"Must have been a hell of a sandwich." He laughs nervously.

"Keep it." I slide a pen at him with more force than I intend and snatch the baggie from the table. These days, I go nowhere without my spoon and baggie; they make me feel close to my Sylvias. Strange, I know, but they comfort me when nobody else can. One miscarriage and you get "Seventy-five percent of women miscarry during their first pregnancy." With the second, it's "My sister/cousin/hairdresser had two; you'll be fine." Three begets "I know of a fertility clinic out in Gaithersburg." I'm on number four.

I return to our apartment and go straight to the guest room I've been avoiding since I lost Sylvia. A stack of pink, blue, and yellow hand-me-downs from Robin provides the only color against the oatmeal carpet and white futon.

Danny's shoved the teak wooden cradle into the corner. We bought it at the Georgetown Flea Market last summer, a few days before our first miscarriage. I remove the spoon and the baggie from my purse and lay them in the cradle. With the edge of my thumb I rock the bassinet back and forth so gently that the spoon and the baggie barely move.

The day folds into itself. At five, I'm massaging a chicken breast with olive oil when Danny calls. "I have to show a house tonight, sweetie. Can I pick up some Ben and Jerry's on the way home?" He sounds both anxious and relieved to take a night off from our grief. I don't blame him. I call my mom in Milwaukee. Just because.

"Whatcha doin'?" I try to sound like that plucky girl who beat the entire sixth grade class in an arm-wrestling tournament, who trotted off to Mali to run an AIDS program, and not the hormonal casualty I am.

"Thinking about you, honey."

"No need."

"We spent today at Aunt Sylvia's house, sorting her things."

My cheeks flush, and I feel like I did when I was eight and my father caught me stealing a piece of Bazooka bubble gum from Winkie's. "Did you find the spoon?"

"The one from your great-grandma Hannah from Minsk?" My mother sounds amused; she's a fourth-generation German Jew and often disparages her mother-in-law's Eastern European ways.

"Yeah," I mumble.

"No sign of it. Right before your grandma Goldie passed, when her dementia got really bad, she went on and on about that spoon and some handkerchief that I've still never seen."

My heart quickens as my mother tells me about a feud between my grandmother and my aunt over this spoon. She's fuzzy about the details, but my grandmother was mad as hell that barren Sylvia kept their mother's baby spoon for herself instead of letting her have it.

I sleep fitfully. I dream that a pregnant Aunt Sylvia eats Neapolitan ice cream with the baby spoon while Grandma Goldie sits in her favorite chair and watches a toddler with braids stand alone on a grassy knoll playing Captain, May I? Raspberries stain the girl's white overalls, and her eyes bulge slightly. The images crash into each other like scenes in an MTV music video.

The next morning, I'm shampooing my hair when I retrieve a memory of the spoon. I was five and a half when my parents let Eric, Amy, and me stay with Aunt Sylvia while they went to the Cayman Islands. She ran us bubble baths and wrapped us in towels that she'd warmed in the dryer. Cocooned in our bathrobes, we curled up on the sofa bed and ate Jiffy Pop. She packed Hostess Ding Dongs in our lunch boxes, and I watched her polish her silver until it sparkled. Only after she finished the candlesticks and kiddush cups did she shine the baby spoon.

On the last day of our stay, I asked her if I could feed my doll with the spoon, which, even as a child, I knew she didn't want me to touch. I also knew that she couldn't say no to me. She nodded toward the spoon, and I grabbed it greedily.

"Here, my little Melanie." I placed the spoon gingerly against the doll's plastic mouth. "My little baby, my baby." I rocked Melanie back and forth. I could feel my aunt watching me, so I hammed it up. "Mommy loves you, Mommy loves you so much." On some level, I knew I was making Aunt Sylvia feel like I did when my brother waved his extended bedtime or gum-chewing privileges in my face. My aunt never polished her silver in front of me again. A year later, I tortured my grandma Goldie with questions about the spoon, but she told me nothing.

To rinse this memory away, I stand under the shower until the water turns cold. I leave a message for my boss telling him that I'm taking off a few more days. I pop my wedding video into the VCR. Danny breaks the glass, and then we kiss as we'd practiced: affectionate but not too much tongue. I fast-forward to Aunt Sylvia, who is fingering a stray rose petal when the camera zooms in on her. She fumbles with the microphone and holds it to her lips, recently touched up with a fresh coat of lipstick. Pink Velvet. Revlon. Funny the things you remember. Her large eyes dart around the room, and she clears her throat several times. "Like someone pulled them off the top of a cake, this bride and groom." She giggles nervously and continues. "My wish for my Hannah is that she know every kind of naches life has to offer." Her laughter fades.

I replay the clip over and over. My aunt is smiling, but her eyes are slightly watery. How could I have missed this? Maybe she suspected that I wasn't going to be able to have children. Maybe she was mourning Uncle Irving. No, he was an asshole; this has to be about me. What possessed me to swipe a fertility totem from a barren woman? How could I have stolen my aunt's birthright?

Tears are forming somewhere in my skull. To stave off

another tidal wave of grief, I drive around the Beltway thinking about my aunt.

"Call me Aunt Sylvia. All the kids do," she told Danny seven years ago when I presented him to her in a dry run for the later round of family introductions. She motioned to a wall of framed photos of my grandmother's progeny while I poked around in her fridge for a Pepsi. She loved to brag about me: "My bat mitzvah...voice like an angel...captain of the volleyball team."

I joined my aunt and Danny in the dining room, where they were laughing at one of his corny jokes. And when I recited the blessings over the candles later that night, I surprised myself with my silent prayer that my walls be filled with photos of my own children and grandchildren.

Ten days post-miscarriage, I pack toiletries, two shirts, and a peasant skirt into a duffel bag; my jeans don't fit because I'm still sporting a sanitary napkin the size of a diaper. I fly Midwest Express to Milwaukee because the seats are roomy and they serve warm chocolate chip cookies and meals with real linen napkins.

A blond woman in her sixties offers me one of her cookies. "I'm Lois. You got family in Milwaukee?"

"I'm visiting a relative."

"You got kids?" She adjusts her Coke-bottle glasses. "Those career women forget to have kids until it's too late and then that's that."

"I have a baby girl." I entertain a confrontation fantasy with

Lois on my way to the bathroom: *Lois, I've lost a baby. I named her Sylvia, and I'm carrying a replica of the fetus made out of raspberry jam and capers in my purse. Would you like to hold her?* The tiny lavatory smells like asparagus pee and jet fuel. I pull the baggie and the spoon out and examine them. Neither one ever truly belonged to me.

I rent a Ford Taurus and drive to Aunt Sylvia's empty colonial house with a For Sale sign planted on the front lawn. I sneak into the backyard and sit cross-legged on her overgrown grass. A ladybug crawls up my big toe. Four raspberries cling to an anemic- looking bush, and I pick them. I open my baggie, which smells vinegary and sweet, and drop in the fruit.

The grass cools my feet as I walk back to the car. While I concentrate on finding my way to the cemetery, I excavate a piece of licorice from the bottom of my purse and run it back and forth between my teeth until it turns into a skinny thread.

Seven white tulips mark Aunt Sylvia's grave. Sylvia Savitz Seigel. What a dreadful name for a woman with a lisp. The thought makes me smile.

I remove my sandals and let my soles sink into the velvety soil. The dirt next to my aunt's grave yields easily as I dig a hole with my fingers. I take the baggie from my purse and place it in the hole. I scoop small chunks of dirt over the plastic with my aunt's spoon, and then I raise its warm handle to my lips and kiss the Hebrew letter *hey*. I drop the heirloom into the earth. A warm breeze tickles me, and I hear a whisper, my whisper.

Yisgadal ve yiskadash shema rabah. Amen.

WHAT HANNAH NEVER KNEW

Goldie Solonsky and Sylvia Seigel, September 1935, 1937, 1970, and 1990

September 1935

Goldie

Of course Goldie Solonsky said yes when her son asked if Hannah, Eric, and baby Amy could spend the night with her. What bubbe would turn away her grandchildren? "I can still make Rosh Hashanah and take care of the kids," she assured Simon. "What do you think I did when you and your sister were children?" She told him that she knew from losing a mother and that his wife needed a little peace and quiet.

This morning her husband, Hyman, had taken Eric, Simon's eldest, to the office to show him off. Eric took after Hyman, gentle, plump, and not so good with the books, but blessed with a knack for listening to people and enough street smarts to find his way, she often reassured Simon, who worried about the boy too much. Hannah, on the other hand, for that one everything came to her on the first try, and Amy, well, she was still a baby so it was too early to tell.

Goldie put Amy down for a nap and began peeling potatoes for her kugel. Hannah sat at the kitchen table sorting her rubber bands by color until she grew bored and asked for a job. "Can I cut the onions, Bubbe?"

"Let's wait until you are seven for that. You'll need all of your fingers to play jacks."

"Can I grate the chocolate for the icebox cake?"

"Your aunt Sylvia will be here soon, cookie. She'll take you across the street and run you around but good."

Hannah pulled a doll from the Milwaukee Sports Club gym bag her father had loaned her for her sleepover. Fancy. The club had just started officially accepting Jews, and her Simon, famous for fixing noses and bosoms, was one of the first to join. Hyman wouldn't have cared about the club even if they'd accepted him. He'd never wanted to shower with the goyim; too many times he'd gotten it for having a different shmeckl.

Hannah fed her doll with a fake bottle. Goldie thought her granddaughter was a bit old for dolls, but what did she know about little girls? Her daughter, Marlene, had run off to San Francisco ten years ago and barely picked up the phone to say hello. Miss Broken Finger.

"Your baby hungry?" Goldie glanced up from a heap of peeled potatoes.

"Yes, Melanie wants Cream of Wheat."

Hannah held her doll to her shoulder with tenderness. This was a child who knew from love. Goldie felt proud of Simon for being such a good father, and proud that he'd picked such a loving wife. So she was bossy, which had only gotten worse when she started burying her nose in those Gloria Steinberg books.

"You're a good mommy, Hannahle."

Hannah's eyes brightened. "Do you have a special spoon too?"

Goldie reached into her top drawer and handed her granddaughter a teaspoon.

"No, Bubbe, a baby spoon." Hannah grabbed the end of one of her pigtails — her hair was black and curly like her father's — split it in two, and tugged.

"My baby is thirty-five years old." Goldie chuckled.

Hannah put her hands on her hips. "Well, Aunt Sylvia doesn't even have kids, and she has a baby spoon."

A chill ran up and down Goldie's back. "What baby spoon?"

"It was small and shiny and silver, and it had a little Hebrew letter on it."

Goldie could tell Hannah was feeling like a real big shot with this piece of grown-up information. "A *hey*," she murmured. Her limbs felt heavy. She wanted to pour herself a glass of ice water and sit down for a second. She had specifically asked Sylvia at Mama's funeral if she'd seen Grandma Hannah's baby spoon, and Sylvia just shook her head in her sweet Sylvia way and said not a word, so Goldie assumed that it had been misplaced. The funeral was more than thirty years ago, but she remembered it as if it were yesterday.

"Are you okay, Bubbe?"

"Of course I'm okay." Goldie's tone was harsher than she

meant it to be. "Bring me that tin. We'll split a pecan bar."

Hannah's eyes, brownish black like Goldie's, grew round. Goldie never interrupted her cooking and baking for anything.

The cookie felt like chalk on Goldie's tongue, but she tried to pretend that a treat was just what the doctor ordered. After everything she'd done, all those envelopes of money, all the fights with Hyman when he insisted that she should just let Sylvia fend for herself, all the times she turned her head the other way when Sylvia's good-for-nothing husband, Irving, showed up in his fine wool suits, all the nights Sylvia spent on Goldie's sofa, all the Shabbat dinners and seders and Rosh Hashanah lunches and the care packages that followed. Not to mention the fact that Sylvia had never so much as invited her over for a grilled cheese sandwich. Why wouldn't Sylvia have wanted Goldie's children and grandchildren — whom she practically pretended were hers sometimes — to take their first bites from the spoon that had touched the mouths of generations of their family's babies? Goldie couldn't even think to peel a potato she was so hot. This one she couldn't blame on Irving.

Hannah examined her bubbe, in that way that made Goldie uneasy, as though her granddaughter were twenty years old already, as though she could see right into Goldie's heart. "Let's go watch for Aunt Sylvia, Bubbe," she suggested in her sweetest voice.

Goldie always felt better when her hands were busy. She led the little girl to her newly reupholstered chair, forest green with gold stripes. "Go get me your hairbrush," she ordered. Hannah returned with the brush and a glass of ice water. "That's a new coffee table. Use a coaster, dear." Hannah placed the glass on a coaster and sat on her knees in front of Goldie, who brushed the tangles out of her hair just as she and Sylvia had done for each other when they shared a bedroom back in Mama's four-room apartment on Burleigh Street.

"There she is, Bubbe!" Hannah pointed out the window to her aunt, still slender and a looker. Hannah had inherited Sylvia's figure, thank God, and not her mother's schmaltz or her father's pear shape that hours of schvitzing in the gym couldn't change. "She's here, she's here! Do you think she brought raspberries?" As Hannah turned around to face her grandmother, Goldie knew what she would read in the little girl's expression. Hannah had never once looked as excited to see her own bubbe as she was to see this woman whom Goldie had thought she knew better than anyone, including Hyman.

Chic in her pantsuit from Gimbel's and her fresh set from Minsky's, Sylvia waved up at Hannah. Goldie's neighbor, Zelda, recovering from her corn surgery, limped to her mailbox and nodded at Sylvia, who kissed her cheek and made a beeline for Goldie's steps.

Goldie hauled herself out of the chair and rushed to her bedroom, where she listened to Hannah's breathless chatter, something about a Barbie doll that talked or some such mishegas. "I'll be out in a second, Sylvia," she called, trying to make her voice sound normal.

Business had been good for Hyman that year. Goldie took her knippel, a fat brown envelope filled with bills she'd been socking away, into the bathroom and sat on the toilet to give herself another minute, but she couldn't stop herself from thinking bad things about her sister. She'd been too generous, and not only with the money. "Simon, have you called your aunt this week?" "Simon, go shovel your aunt's front step." "Simon, take the kids to see Sylvia; they need to know their aunt." "Sylvia, you play with the kids. I'll fiddle around in the kitchen."

Goldie was sobbing now, and the tears were going to give her away. Once she started, though, she just couldn't stop. She would frighten Hannah, who, like Sylvia, missed nothing. She buried her face in a bath towel until her shoulders stopped shaking. Cold water helped, but she would need a miracle to hide her puffy face.

Sylvia knocked on the door. "Goldie, you okay in there?"

"Just a little indigestion. Take Hannah to the park."

"You sure? You don't sound so good."

"Go."

When Goldie heard the door close, she came out of the bathroom and began chopping potatoes again. Halfway through the second potato, Sylvia and Hannah returned for Hannah's doll. Goldie just wanted to keep chopping, but for the sake of her Hannah, she had to force a smile. Sylvia looked worried, and Hannah looked scared. Goldie's eyes were so swollen that they felt like buttonholes in her head.

"Come on, my little monkey. Come and show me your trick on the bars." Sylvia stroked one of Hannah's plaits and guided her out the door.

The envelope felt heavy in the pocket of Goldie's slacks. Part of her wanted to look her sister square in the eye and hand her the money, instead of her usual pretending that it just appeared like magic in Sylvia's pocketbook. Part of her wanted to keep the money and splurge on a trip to Florida with Hyman next winter. Most of her wanted to turn back the clock, to tell Mama that Sylvia was the older one and she should take care of herself, or maybe even Goldie, once in a while.

Goldie finished peeling her potato, then reached for another and another. After she added egg and flour and onion to the bowl of chopped potatoes, she grabbed Sylvia's purse from the kitchen table, returned to her window chair, and zipped the envelope into the side compartment of her sister's bag. She watched Hannah and Sylvia emerge from behind the big slide in the middle of the park; Sylvia put out her hand, and Hannah grabbed it. From the way they tilted their heads, Goldie knew they were sharing a laugh, a good giggle. And nobody knew better than Goldie how warm it felt on the inside of Sylvia's laughter.

September 1935

Goldie

Goldie thought she might plotz if she had to wait one more second to tell Sylvia the big news. Every few minutes, she peered out her living room window, waiting for her sister to come help her prepare her first Rosh Hashanah feast.

She fluffed her new chair, delivered fresh from Zellen's Furniture Store just in time for this important lunch. If Sylvia ever got here, she would help whip up cabbage rolls, three kinds of kugel, brisket, and of course Mama's icebox cake. The men would eat until their paunches strained against their belts, and the aunties would squirm in their girdles, pledging to eat bread and water for days after the meal. But Goldie and

Hyman wouldn't announce their news to the family, not yet, too soon.

She could see everything from the new chair, including willowy Sylvia finally waltzing down the street. Rays of sunshine poked through an umbrella of elm trees, catching the reds and golds in her hair as she moved in and out of the light. Her narrow shoulders drooped from lugging shopping bags brimming with last-minute items Goldie had asked her to pick up at Saltzberg's.

Marshall Plotkin broke from a game of kick-the-can to give Sylvia a big hello. She used to babysit for half the boys on the west side of Milwaukee before she married that Irving. Back then, Goldie didn't share her sister's enthusiasm for children; she preferred to meet her girlfriends at Walgreen's to gossip over chocolate phosphates and French fries. But now, everything had changed. Goldie was going to be a mother.

Zelda Greenberg waddled out of the bottom half of Goldie and Hyman's duplex and stopped Sylvia to look into her grocery bags. Sylvia, too polite to end the conversation, smiled and nodded for what seemed like hours while Zelda nattered on, probably kvetching about her corns; she was always kvetching about something.

By the time Sylvia let herself into the kitchen, Goldie's impatience had gotten the better of her. She got up, fluffed the indentation of her body from the chair, and walked toward the kitchen.

"You're too nice to Zelda Greenberg, she probably asked you how much you paid Saltzberg for the groceries. She's got real nose trouble," Goldie said as she pulled a place setting

for Zelda from the breakfront in her dining room. Calmer
now that her sister was here, she savored the anticipation of
sharing her secret, just like she used to love sharing a string of
black licorice at the matinee.

Sylvia retrieved a pound of ground beef and a bunch of
parsley from a shopping bag and placed them on Goldie's
kitchen table. "Isn't collecting strays what you're supposed
to do on Rosh Hashanah?" She started giggling; her laughter,
thick as honey, filled the room.

"What? What's funny?"

"Birdie Finkelstein's cement cakes."

Goldie couldn't contain her smile; she could never stay
sore at Sylvia for long. "Mama said Birdie dropped one of her
honey cakes on her foot and broke her toe."

Goldie and Sylvia shared a good laugh.

"I've got a surprise for you." Sylvia set a bowl on the
counter. "From my garden."

"A farmer we've got in the family." Goldie peeled away the
tinfoil and nearly gasped at the mound of perfectly shaped
raspberries. "We'll put them in the applesauce."

"Whatever you like." Sylvia's eyes — Mama's eyes, gray and
slightly bulging — shone with pride.

Goldie couldn't hold in her news any longer; she patted her belly and smiled big. "You're not the only one with a
surprise."

Sylvia paused for a second, and then her eyes widened
and she pulled Goldie to her body and hugged her tight. "Mazel tov, mazel tov." She sniffled.

Tears of joy. This was exactly how Goldie wanted it to be

when she told her sister she had killed the rabbit. She reached deep into the pocket of her housedress and pulled out the crisp white handkerchief Sylvia had given her for her last birthday.

Sylvia examined the embroidered pink roses and inscription: *Always, Sylvia.* "It's too pretty to use."

"Go ahead, blow already. We've got work to do."

Sylvia blotted her upper lip, leaving a small dot of pink lipstick. "I'll take it home and wash."

Neither sister would speak another word about the baby. Mama had always warned them that gloating, or even discussing their good fortune, was a sure way to attract the evil eye, especially when it came to babies. Goldie used to think this was mishegas from the old country, but best to be careful anyway. She certainly wouldn't dare mention Grandma Hannah's sterling silver baby spoon, smuggled from Minsk. Goldie had always figured that Sylvia would have the first baby because she was older, so she'd get the spoon first, but now Mama would give Goldie the spoon after the first baby came, of course, and she and Sylvia would pass it between them. Like Grandma Hannah and Mama, like Goldie and Sylvia, all the babies in the family would take their first bites from this treasure.

Goldie took her sister's cool hand. "Come, let's start on the cabbage rolls already. Once Hyman comes home, he'll want what to eat, and that will be that." She gave Sylvia a head of cabbage and plopped the ground beef in a cast-iron skillet.

"How many people will we be?" Sylvia asked, cutting out the core of the cabbage with a long knife.

"You and Irving made twelve, and now Nosy Pants Zelda,

that's thirteen."

Sylvia cast her eyes down and began separating cabbage leaves. "Irving can't...Irving's not coming."

"What?" Goldie put her hands on her hips, steadying herself against a fresh wave of Irving anger.

Sylvia smoothed out the cabbage leaves with her slender fingers. "His boss don't know from Rosh Hashanah." She spooned ground beef into the flattened leaves and folded them into envelopes.

"Twelve, then. One batch will be plenty." Goldie pursed her lips as she retrieved a large pot from her bottom cabinet. "Here, help me with the sauce." She handed Sylvia two cans of tomatoes and a can opener.

Sylvia stared at the beige linoleum tiles and shifted her weight from one foot to the other. "I won't be coming either. Irving doesn't want I should go by myself."

Goldie felt like Sylvia had slapped her. How could her own sister not show for her first Rosh Hashanah feast? A thick silence hung between them as Goldie diced an onion. The smell tore through the kitchen like a brush fire.

Sylvia minced garlic and parsley, passing the correct amount of each ingredient to Goldie, as both sisters had always done for their mother when she cooked and baked.

"Keep stirring. It's too gloppy. I'll be back in a minute," Goldie said, and handed her wooden spoon over to Sylvia.

Sitting on the sliver between the twin beds she and Hyman had pushed together to make their queen, Goldie pondered her embarrassment of riches: a baby on the way, Mama's first grandchild to eat from Grandma Hannah's spoon, a bread-winner like Hyman who made a good living even during a depression and remembered to buy his wife a box of choco-lates for her birthday, and now the honor of preparing Rosh Hashanah lunch. What did Sylvia have? A no-goodnik Ir-ving. Who cared if he looked like Errol Flynn? He liked his schnapps too much, and his "deals." He was probably in trou-ble again, didn't want to face Uncle Seymour. Probably owed him money.

It had always been this way with scrawny Sylvia. Mama had told Goldie that she was the strong one and that she had to watch out for Sylvia. In kindergarten, Goldie — just a grade behind Sylvia — beat Sari Coppel up for calling her sister Bug Eyes and teasing her about her slight lisp. Mama scolded Goldie for fighting, but Goldie knew that she didn't really mean it. She never felt more proud of herself than when she fought her sister's battles.

She stuck her hand under Hyman's mattress and pulled out her knippel. So the baby wouldn't have the fanciest buggy on Fifty-first Street. An ugly memory jumped into Goldie's head. The one time Hyman said that Irving might actually get rich from one of his "deals," something to do with liquor. Goldie hadn't felt happy for her sister at all.

She returned to the kitchen to find Sylvia arranging cab-bage rolls in a pan.

"That's a nice batch," she said, and slid the brown envelope into the pocket of her sister's dress.

"I…we…can't." Sylvia bit her lip.

"Mahjongg. You know I'm a big shot with the tiles. Come. Brew a cup of coffee for the icebox cake."

"Irving is picking me up in a few minutes. I'll make the cake at my house and bring it over."

"A few minutes?" Goldie's heart sank again. This was not turning out anything like she had planned. Her morning with Sylvia was ruined, thanks to Irving.

"Maybe I can come for Rosh Hashanah. I'll ask again," Sylvia offered.

Goldie shrugged.

Sylvia touched her index finger lightly against Goldie's belly. "Mazel tov," she said again, and tears sprang to her eyes.

In spite of her disappointment, Goldie was moved. She ran hot water over the greasy skillet until she could no longer hear Sylvia's heels clicking against the linoleum steps that led to the landing of the duplex. Wiping her hands on a towel, she returned to her new chair and peeked out the window. Irving stood at the gate, grinning at Sylvia. So cocky, that one. And too handsome. Sylvia caressed Irving's cheek with one hand and with the other stuffed the fat envelope into the breast pocket of his finely tailored suit. He slipped his arm around her shoulders, which now drooped under the weight of a new debt.

September 1937

Sylvia

Sylvia's feet swelled in her pumps — Irving didn't approve of those frumpy tie-up shoes, even for a cooking day — as she trekked an extra seven blocks to buy bananas for Goldie's toddler, Simon, along with a few "while you're there pick me up some..." items. The handles of her shopping bags left red creases in her fingers, and her shoulders ached.

Even before she married a man who couldn't afford to spend two months of grocery money on a brisket, Sylvia had known that she would never make Rosh Hashanah, even though she was the eldest. Let Goldie have the spotlight — she'd practically begged Mama to allow her to recite all four questions the first Passover she knew how to read. Sylvia's stomach burned, though, when she thought about Goldie's first Rosh Hashanah feast, and how she'd schlepped to Saltzberg's when she should have stayed in bed recovering from her miss. So much blood she'd lost. Ten weeks, she figured from the womanly calendar she kept in her jewelry box. She had thought about telling Goldie, but how could she? Goldie was bursting with her own news; she was carrying little Simon. Sylvia was happy for her sister, but God strike her dead for not being able to bear Goldie's big smiles over her perfect kugels and the new life growing inside her. She'd fasted for an extra hour that Yom Kippur for lying to her sister about Irving making her stay home from the lunch.

Rosh Hashanah used to be Sylvia's favorite holiday. Mama and her sisters would begin planning the menu the minute Uncle Seymour wolfed down the last Passover macaroon. And then, the week before the first night of Rosh Hashanah, Sylvia would help her mother polish the silver, wiping the metal until it turned shiny. She loved presenting Mama with a sparkling kiddush cup or candlestick.

Sylvia caressed the slender handle of the spoon in her

pocket; its metal ridge moved up and down against her leg as she walked. Goldie was expecting her second child on Thanksgiving Day, and Sylvia knew she should have given her sister Grandma Hannah's baby spoon for Simon. Soon Sylvia would turn thirty, too old for babies. Besides, Irving said no more trying; two accidents, that was enough. He sent his girl Katie Flanagan from the office to teach Sylvia about the rhythm method. The nerve. She knew he used to shtup Katie before he and Sylvia got serious. She swallowed her humiliation, felt it lodge in her stomach, where Dr. Klein told her that an ulcer was forming.

"Heads up, Sammy!" The sound of Marshall Plotkin's manboy voice interrupted her thoughts. She watched him throw a baseball to one of his friends. So big they'd gotten. Marshall would be embarrassed if the lady who used to wipe his tush bothered him when he was with his friends, although she did catch his eye and smile.

She glanced up through the elm trees, and sure enough Goldie was waiting at her post, her fancy chair, with Simon on her lap. Just to utz her little sister, Sylvia gave Goldie's downstairs neighbor, Zelda Greenberg, an extra-warm smile, and poor widowed Zelda, whom Goldie had no patience for, climbed all over her. Zelda wasn't so bad. Sylvia wanted to offer to help her pluck her eyebrows; she'd shaped one so oddly that it always looked raised.

"Nu, Sylvia, that sister of yours got you running around town?" Zelda glanced inside Sylvia's shopping bags and then snuck a quick peek at Sylvia's flat belly, her questioning eyebrow arching further toward the top of her head.

"Happy New Year to you, Zelda." Sylvia climbed up the steps to Goldie's door, now wanting to be rid of Zelda altogether.

Goldie greeted her sister with an extra place setting for Zelda in her hands. "Did she at least offer to bring anything this year?"

"You can invite her if you want." Sylvia spoke without emotion. The last thing she needed was Zelda staring at her belly all afternoon.

Goldie gave her a look but said nothing.

"Come here, my little Simon." Sylvia plunked down her bags and took her nephew in her arms. "I brought you a banana."

Goldie rubbed her belly. "I'm going to put him down for his nap."

"Go nap yourself. Tell me what's left to make."

When Sylvia opened the Frigidaire to put away the groceries, she saw that Goldie had already prepared the cabbage rolls, kugels, and briskets. What was she trying to prove, that one?

Goldie reappeared in the kitchen and smiled sheepishly. "In case the baby should come early. I'm already so big; I had to take off my rings." She held up her fingers, normally fleshy, now as swollen as little kishkes.

Sylvia shook her head, but she couldn't help feeling a surge of love toward her sister. So pigheaded and strong and generous. Too often these warm feelings escaped through what Dr. Klein called "the hole" in her stomach, making room for jealousy over Goldie's babies and her sweet, honest Hyman Solonsky. Sylvia could never have married an immigrant, much less someone with pockmarks and an underbite. And so serious! He worked like an animal selling insurance. His debit routes were successful because he had this way of listening to a person like what they said was important, and he did right by Goldie, and that was what mattered.

"Come, I haven't made the icebox cake yet." Goldie nodded toward the Frigidaire.

"It's a good day to make meringue, not too humid."

"You got eggs?" Goldie asked just as Simon started to cry.

"Go. I'll start the cake."

Sylvia took the spoon out of her pocket. She had shined it up good for Goldie, rubbing her felt cloth around the bowl — just big enough to fit into a baby's little pink mouth — then down the long, skinny neck to the handle, where she slid the cloth onto the engraved Hebrew letter *hey*, the first letter in Grandma Hannah's name. She could practically hear her mother's words: "Your grandmother Hannah, allah vashalom, smuggled this in her petticoats. It's yours, for your baby." She'd opened Sylvia's hand and placed the spoon in her palm. But that was before Goldie's pregnancy and the rhythm method and Katie Flanagan and Sylvia's discovery that Irving didn't want to work for anything, even a baby. Mama died before she found out that Goldie was pregnant with Simon, probably assuming that Sylvia would eventually bear her a grandchild. Better that Mama not know from her daughter's trouble.

Sylvia stuffed the spoon back into her pocket, took out Mama's old green mixing bowl, and began pulling ingredients from Goldie's cupboards: flour, sugar, vanilla, chocolate, soda. The hand grater she used to sliver the chocolate dug into her fingers, already sore from lugging the shopping bags. When Goldie came in and rested a warm hand on Sylvia's back, Sylvia caught a whiff of the pickled herring on her sister's breath and Simon's toddler drool on her clothes; the smells were strong, yet innocent, just like Goldie. Her face, normally heart-shaped and full, looked doughy and red. The corner of a brown envelope poked out of the pocket of her housedress.

Sylvia thought about the yellow silk shift she'd seen in the window of Gimbel's and how perfect it would look for the holidays with the matching hat and bag. Or they could buy a new davenport; the springs of their pullout were practically bruising her thin legs every time she sat down. But she didn't have the nerve to make herself a knippel; she knew she would slip the money into Irving's pocket, next to a napkin with some tootsie's lipstick kiss. She'd pretend that the money just found its way there, that this endless borrowing didn't cost her. In blood. And for a while he would make her feel like his Sylvie again.

She looked away when Goldie slipped the envelope into Sylvia's pocketbook. Part of her wanted to tell Goldie that she was doing just fine, thank you very much, and that she didn't need her sister's charity, and that Goldie could run her own errands from now on. But out of the corner of her eye, she also noticed that the envelope looked a little slimmer than usual.

Sylvia fought the urge to assure Goldie that Irving had a big deal cooking and he'd pay her back soon. She slid her left hand into the pocket of her dress, burrowing her fingers deep into the satin lining to stroke the spoon, and reached for the sifter with her right; the flour fell like snow into the mixing bowl, green as Katie Flanagan's eyes.

September 1990

Sylvia

It was the third Rosh Hashanah after Irving died before Sylvia found herself back on Goldie's street, now treeless thanks to that Dutch elm business. Irving's stroke was as good a reason as any for Sylvia to drift from Goldie's life; she had spent fifteen years feeding him applesauce and toileting him. Like a baby.

Broken glass and greasy McDonald's bags littered the playground where she'd once watched Simon play kick-the-can and Hannah and Amy swing across the bars like monkeys. A Hmong woman wearing a Green Bay Packers sweatshirt nodded to her as she checked what Sylvia would always regard as Zelda Greenberg's mailbox. A little girl, probably the woman's granddaughter, played cat's cradle with an old shoelace on the steps.

Sylvia never thought she'd miss Zelda, just as she didn't realize how much she'd missed Goldie until Simon called last week to tell her that his mother was getting confused, that the fire department had come twice to her duplex after she'd gone to bed with a kugel in the oven, that he'd hired a nurse to make sure that she ate and bathed, that there might not be too many good conversations with Goldie left.

She was glad Simon had called. Both Simon and his son Eric had inherited Hyman's bad skin and good heart. For the past fifteen years, the first of the month had always brought that thin envelope addressed to "Aunt Sylvia Savitz" in Simon's doctor's scrawl. Sylvia could never repay Goldie, or Simon for that matter, for all the money they'd given her over the years, but she had another idea. Her pocketbook dangled from her forearm, slapping her hip as she walked. Zipped safely in the side pocket, wrapped in one of Mama's old handkerchiefs, was the freshly polished baby spoon, her peace offering to Goldie. She would give it to her right away.

All those years of schlepping Irving around had given Sylvia a bad back, which now ached from walking four blocks with the bags holding her Rosh Hashanah feast: cabbage rolls, kishke, a brisket, an icebox cake, and a few raspberries from her backyard. She climbed the steps to Goldie's duplex, that old burn in her gut catching fire just from thinking about what had to be done. When she let herself into the kitchen, she was rattled to find a bag of Dunkin' Donuts and an old coffee cup on the counter. The potato bowl sat empty. Mama had taught Goldie and Sylvia to always keep a potato or two in the house to fill out a meal. The kitchen smelled clean, though — maybe too clean.

"In here, Heidi," Goldie called out from the living room. "Did you pick up the chocolate chips?"

Heidi must be her help. Just like Goldie to order people to the grocery store. Sylvia smiled, relieved that her sister was up to her usual tricks, took a deep breath, and went into the living room, which smelled as her own had during Irving's last year, like fish and antiseptic.

Goldie looked as if her old chair — threadbare and faded to

a mustard green — might swallow her up. Her arthritic hands sat folded on her lap, and as she shifted her weight, the plastic cover made a crinkling noise under her shrunken frame.

"Sylvia?" Goldie smiled like a child opening her first Hanukkah present, too surprised to show the practiced cold shoulder she'd been perfecting these past years.

"I brought you a few things." Sylvia was still holding the shopping bags.

Goldie stared at her sister, grinning, adjusting her loose housedress, revealing her bony shoulders and freckled skin. "You know Viola Schnitz died. Dropped dead. Heart attack," she said, as if she'd seen Sylvia just yesterday. She patted her chest.

Viola Schnitz had been dead for thirteen years, but maybe Goldie was just trying to make things easier. "Such a shame," Sylvia said. Safer to talk about Viola than other things.

"She was as big as a house when she went. You never saw her that way, but I'm telling you, she must have been eating yeast."

Goldie hadn't changed one bit. "She used to be movie-star gorgeous," Sylvia said.

"Yeast, I tell you." Goldie shook her head. "She used to be movie-star gorgeous."

"I got you a present." Sylvia set a bag of black licorice from the Pic 'n Save on the coffee table. Goldie and the help must drink a lot of coffee; rings from their mugs had ruined the table, the one that arrived right before Goldie hosted one of the last Rosh Hashanah lunches Sylvia attended. Goldie was so worried that this silly piece of furniture wouldn't come in time for her to show it off to the family.

Goldie grabbed the licorice bag and settled it on her lap.

"How are the kids?" Sylvia asked.

"Simon's getting married. Brenda. German Jew." Goldie smiled with pride. "A bit of a snob."

Simon and Brenda had been married for more than thirty years. Goldie's confusion ripped at Sylvia's heart. Sure, things hadn't always been easy with her sister, but Goldie had always been the rock, the bank, the fierce little girl who socked anyone who dared poke fun at Sylvia's lisp.

"You know, she looks just like you did back then, long and willowy," Goldie announced.

"Your Hannah is much prettier than I was." Sylvia could always follow her sister's thoughts, even now, when it seemed like someone had put them in a pot of soup and stirred them up good. Sylvia hadn't noticed how alike she and Hannah looked until she was rifling through old pictures last week, and she didn't much like the comparison. She wanted more naches out of life for her great-niece. It made her ache to know that Hannah was having trouble making babies too. Now, Amy, she was built like Goldie, peasant-like, short with a bosom, and mischievous and light, a real artist, but still a child that one.

"What else did you bring?" Goldie looked in the direction of the bags.

"Cabbage rolls, brisket, kishke, icebox cake, a few raspberries from the yard," Sylvia answered; she wanted Goldie's Rosh Hashanah to be perfect. "Simon picked out the finest cut from the kosher butcher out by him and Brenda."

Goldie's attention drifted; her eyes, once dark and bright, were grayish and watery. She patted the arm of the davenport that butted up against her chair. "Come, sit."

Sylvia stepped around her bags and sat as close to Goldie as she could. Goldie's breath smelled like dirty flower water, and coarse, dark hairs sprouted from her chin.

"That's better," Goldie said.

They sat together in silence for a few minutes. Sylvia took a deep breath, thinking Goldie wouldn't notice.

"Nu, what's on your mind, Sylvia, after all these years?" She was the old Goldie.

"I have something for you," Sylvia said softly.

"I see, all that food. Simon will come with the kids, and we'll have a feast tomorrow." She paused. "You'll be with us." It was a statement, not a question.

"No, not the food." As Sylvia was getting up to retrieve her handbag from the kitchen, she felt Goldie's fingers pressing into her arm through her thin sweater.

"Stay," her sister commanded. "Hyman loves your icebox cake. He would wump up half of it if I didn't stop him."

Hyman had been dead for ten years. "A good eater you married."

"Twenty-five cents."

Sylvia knew Goldie was talking about some kind of bargain from Saltzberg's, which had been replaced by a discount shoe store twenty years ago.

"Twelve ounces of chocolate for twenty-five cents at Saltzberg's. Dial up Zelda for me, dear. LOCUST-2424."

"Mrs. Nosy Pants."

"If I don't invite her, she'll mope around tomorrow and tell me that she fixed herself a ham sandwich and a warm glass of cola and listened to our family make such a racket that she couldn't take her nap." Goldie frowned.

"That one." Sylvia shook her head, almost convincing herself that Zelda was still utzing both of them, though she had died five years ago. Sylvia wished they could travel back to a time when Zelda was their biggest headache.

"I'll ask her to bring a potato kugel. She makes a decent kugel." Goldie brightened with the germ of a new idea. "And maybe she'll pick up some chocolate chips for me at Saltzberg's. Twenty-five cents."

The tarnished silver, Heidi the help's dreck on the counter, the nylon knee-highs falling down Goldie's bony white legs — it all reminded Sylvia of a darkened movie set after all the actors had returned to their regular lives, the props too worn to recycle.

"Otherwise, she's not so ai–yi–yi in the kitchen. Did I tell you that Viola Schnitz passed away?"

"A shame."

"Heart attack. I've got new neighbors downstairs. Orientals. Big Packers fans, just like Hyman."

Sylvia wanted the spoon in her hand so she could just give it to Goldie if she came back to the here and now. Sylvia wanted to take back all the years she'd been sore at her sister. What had made her so mad anyway? "Just a second, Goldie. I'm going to put the food in the Frigidaire."

Goldie nodded toward the kitchen.

Goldie's fridge had never been so naked: a carton of

yogurt, Velveeta cheese for the help, a few bruised apples, and some butterscotch pudding. Sylvia took the spoon out of her purse, slid it up her sleeve, and went back to the living room.

Goldie looked worn out as she gazed listlessly toward the park, at the Hmong grandmother sipping orange soda pop and the granddaughter skipping rope on Simon's old basketball court, her purple hair ribbon bobbing up and down in perfect time with her feet.

"Listen to me, Goldie."

"You think I'm not listening?" She glanced at Sylvia, then back out the window.

Sylvia knew that glance, the glance toward the street that Sylvia stopped traveling when things got bad with Irving. "You've done good by me, Goldie." She felt the spoon against her wrist. "You and Simon."

"You're my Sylvia." Goldie stated this as fact and stared straight ahead. "No matter what."

Sylvia began pulling the spoon from her sleeve, and Goldie's head snapped toward her.

"For Hannah," Goldie announced with finality, brushing her crooked thumb against Sylvia's sweater, grazing the hard metal.

"You give it to her," Sylvia replied gently. She extended the spoon, and the shiny silver hung between them, charged with enough electricity to light up every lamp in the apartment.

Goldie touched the stem lightly, then pushed the spoon back toward Sylvia. "I could forget," she said, her voice full with a joke, her eyes — smart, amused, bright — smiling at Sylvia. She winked, and then they giggled, softly at first, then loud and big, then deeper and deeper, from buried places: Mama's Rosh Hashanah table where Birdie Finkelstein bent a butter knife trying to slice her honey cake. Grandma Hannah's dresser stuffed with badly made wigs that they tugged over their braids. Cool spring nights when they crawled under the covers of the twin mattress they shared and gossiped about Hershel Klein's pickle breath. Hot Rosh Hashanah mornings when they sprang out of bed to dress Mama's icebox cake with whipped cream and maraschino cherries. Snowy February days when they woke up with frozen noses and breath that smoked. Huddled together for warmth, they'd listen for Mama's last noodge and then yank back the yellowed goose-down comforter from the old country and leap into the cruel winter morning.

A tear formed somewhere in the bottom of Sylvia's throat, but it never found her eyes. She poked around in her sweater sleeve for a tissue, just in case it did. Without looking at Sylvia, Goldie reached into her own sleeve and handed her sister a yellowed handkerchief.

Sylvia's heart filled up so full that she thought it might pop like a balloon. She felt Goldie watching as she spread the handkerchief on her lap and placed the spoon in the center. Before she folded the material around it, she paused to finger the faded pink embroidered roses and the inscription: *Always, Sylvia.*

SKIN
Eric Solonsky, October 1995

On a warm Yom Kippur afternoon, Eric Solonsky stood on his front lawn, waiting for a delivery of Thai food and listening to the birds converse. A blade of overgrown grass brushed his ankle as he imagined his sisters, Hannah and Amy, and the rest of his family fasting and beating their breasts for a year's worth of sins in the main sanctuary of Hannah's synagogue.

He handed a twenty to a young man wearing an oversized Old Navy T-shirt and took a deep breath before returning to his in-laws and an exhausted Maggie, who was trying with a patient fervor to get their newborn to nurse. Eric felt useless in the pursuit, so he loitered for a few more minutes in the scraggly yard of 1935 East Bertrand Court, down payment compliments of his father. Maintaining a lawn, shopping at a store called Buy Buy Baby, ordering takeout on Yom Kippur, not to mention gathering thirty people, including his gentile in-laws, to watch his son's penis get whacked tomorrow at noon — it all seemed a little surreal.

He entered the house quietly through the back door and

found Alec swaddled like a burrito, sleeping on top of Maggie's chest.

"He ate," Maggie's mother mouthed. Maggie's parents had flown in from Milwaukee the day before Alec's birth.

Eric grinned at his wife, gave her a thumbs-up, and pointed to the brown paper bag of food in his hand. Without rousing Alec, Maggie managed to get up from the couch and lower him into the bassinet they'd set up in the family room. He'd left a spit-up stain the shape of Florida on her T-shirt, and one of her engorged breasts was nearly double the size of its partner. Loose flesh encased her middle, pimples covered her chin, and blue veins popped out of her calves. Eric had spent his senior year of high school, back in Milwaukee, fantasizing about Maggie Stramm's loveliness, and he still saw her as the cheerleader whose finely sculpted nostrils flared as she rooted for boys with athletic ability and smooth skin. Maggie hadn't remembered him ten years later when she saw him playing bass with a U2 cover band at an Earth Day fundraiser on Capitol Hill.

"Are you sure you don't want to stay?" Eric asked Maggie's mother, dutifully. "Looks like they gave us an extra order of pineapple fried rice."

"Oh, gosh, I'm not an adventurous eater, although Will and I do go for chop suey now and then. What was the name of that Oriental family who went to your high school?"

Maggie bit. "Asian, Mom. They were Asian."

"Oh, Maggie. Asian, African American, American Indian... Who can keep up? Eric, do you remember them?" Helene smiled at him.

"The Kimuras. They were Japanese, I think," he answered.

No doubt, Helene said these things to rile Maggie, who worked for a diversity training company whose CEO regularly pinched her ass, but Eric guessed that Helene would have added Jews to the list if she were sipping her zinfandel at the club. In the heat of the wedding planning, Maggie had relayed Helene's comment that if she had to marry a Jew, she could at least have picked a lawyer or a doctor. He rationalized that Helene's comments were no worse than his mother's occasional remark about "those goyim and their cocktails."

"Helene, let's let them get some rest," Will urged, suitcase in hand.

Right about now, Eric's parents, also in town for the bris, were probably perspiring in their High Holiday wools and linens, chatting in the shadow of the enormous menorah outside the temple. They always took a break at one or one-thirty, right after Musaf.

Will kissed Maggie's cheek. "We're going to meander down to the World War II Memorial before we head over to Amy's."

Amy was a saint for putting up Maggie's parents. "Call it a thank-you gift for that killer apartment, big brother," she'd said of the apartment overlooking the zoo that Maggie and Eric had bequeathed to her.

Helene slid her purse up her arm, toned from hours on the tennis court, and snuck another peek at Alec. "I hate to run off when I could make another casserole or help you with the laundry."

Helene had spent the past week knitting, whipping up

concoctions involving Campbell's soup products, and telling
nonstop anecdotes about Maggie's first days of life, while Will
busied himself assembling baby gliders, swings, and strollers.

"Oh, no, Mom," Maggie said. "Please, you've done enough.
Go see the sights."

After they said their goodbyes, Eric and Maggie took their
Thai food into the kitchen and sat down at the Ikea table Eric
had moved from apartment to apartment and finally this
house.

"You okay?" he asked.

She rested her head on his shoulder. "Do you know what
my mother told me? 'I got back into my size four weeks after I
had you, dear.' "

"Oh, babe."

"And back then a size four was a real four!" Maggie looked
in the direction of the den, where Alec was sleeping. "I promise never to count your calories, buddy," she said, tearing into
a carton of drunken noodles.

Eric registered the sounds of Maggie swallowing, Alec
breathing through his stuffy little nose, the hum of the fluorescent kitchen lights — occupational hazard. He worked as an
audio technician.

Maggie was eating so fast she was barely chewing. "You
ordered these from Spices?" she asked through a mouthful of
noodles.

"Only the best for the mother of my son." They'd been doing a lot of this third- person kind of talk since the baby was
born.

She gobbled up the rest of the order without speaking,

spearing the last fat noodle with her fork. Then she said, "My parents don't get the bris thing."

"Did you tell them that we're going to have him baptized too?" Eric asked.

She tossed the empty carton into the trash. "Of course. I tried to explain that a bris is a highly significant Jewish rite of passage rooted in a tradition thousands of years old, but achieving cultural competency isn't exactly their life's mission." When Maggie was agitated, she peppered her speech with diversity-training jargon, nodding her head authoritatively at the end of every sentence.

"It will be over tomorrow." He was eager to end the conversation.

"But I certainly wasn't going to tell them how hard it was to find a mole who would circumcise a baby with a Methodist mother," she said, as if he hadn't spoken.

"Mole" was how she pronounced mohel, no matter how many times he'd said, "rhymes with boil, honey." Whenever Maggie mentioned either the bris or the baptism, it was like having the barber part his hair on the wrong side of his head.

"Why don't you treat yourself to a nice hot shower while the baby's sleeping?" he suggested.

Maggie sighed, kissed him on the forehead, and trotted upstairs to the bathroom..

Eric tried to doze on the couch. While Helene and Will were taking in the new war memorial, his parents were probably enduring the hardest stretch of the fast, the two o'clock headache and grouchiness. For the first time since he married Maggie, he thought about the Yom Kippurs he'd spent as a kid, the mid-afternoon fights Amy picked with Hannah, and the sanctuary that reeked of the bad breath of hundreds of fasters who had gathered to hear the shofar, the signal that this day of torture was over. On the drive to Grandma Goldie's house, Eric and his sisters used to guzzle orange juice and wolf graham crackers, a warm-up for the table of bagels, lox spread, marble cake, and Aunt Sylvia's faithful pan of macaroni and cheese.

A wail interrupted the gentle ache creeping up on him, and Maggie rushed downstairs and swooped up Alec.

Eric stood over the glider, stroking Maggie's damp hair; Alec's jaw moved up and down furiously, and his tiny hand rested atop her breast. "Looks like he's getting the hang of it."

Maggie nodded, gazing at Alec's profile. The phone rang, startling him, and he spit out a mouthful of milk and started to cry.

Eric grabbed the receiver.

"We're at Hannah's. What a ballabuste, as your grandma Goldie would have said," Eric's mother announced. "She even made that god-awful icebox cake for the bris."

Eric laughed, and his mother put his father on the line.

"You want to stop by?" Eric detected the urgency in Simon's voice. He knew that his father wanted nothing more than for the family to break the fast together.

Eric begged off, claiming the baby needed rest for his big day tomorrow, and stretched his arms out to Maggie, who handed over Alec.

"So did your parents give you a big guilt trip about not 'breaking the fast' with them?" She made air quotes with her fingers.

He was expected to reply with some disparaging comment about Simon and Brenda, because this was how they spoke of each other's parents to one another —Maggie and Eric against the world— but he couldn't bring himself to do it today. "They understood."

"Did you tell them how perfectly the fine chefs at Spices prepared your Yom Kippur shrimp?" She giggled meanly.

"I think our little guy has a present for us." He felt the baby's wet warmth under his hand. "I'll take him upstairs and change him."

Eric was relieved to have a moment alone with Alec. Maggie so rarely got on his nerves. He didn't mind the Christmas tree she plunked in the living room last December, or the ham and chocolate bunnies she served to a tableful of her friends last spring, but this bris talk felt different. Bad different. Uncomfortable different. He and Maggie had married quickly, out of passion, against their parents' wishes. They assured everyone that they'd figure out this interfaith stuff, that Maggie understood better than anyone how to merge two cultures.

When he came back downstairs, he saw that Maggie had leaked breast milk on the T-shirt she'd borrowed from him. He jumped at her request to run to the mall and pick up some nursing pads.

Eric felt insanely Jewish trolling through Montgomery Mall on Yom Kippur. He surveyed the array of shoppers, taking note of the varieties of blond: a highlighted soccer mom lugging a huge Crate and Barrel shopping bag, a dishwater twentysomething manning an electronics kiosk, a towheaded toddler wearing the remnants of a chocolate ice cream cone on her chin. Would Alec inherit Maggie's hair? Would he turn out dark-haired, pockmarked, and irreversibly chubby, like the Solonsky men?

A heavily perfumed saleswoman smiled at him when he walked into Mimi Maternity in search of breast pads. After discussing Maggie's cup size at excruciating length, they picked out their best estimate of the right-size pads.

He wandered down to Sears to look for a lawn mower. Why not? He'd tried to convince himself that his unkempt lawn hadn't embarrassed him when his dad pulled up to the house the day before. He wouldn't have felt as ashamed had he been able to cover the entire down payment. God, this was the first time he'd taken money from his father since high school. He'd sworn that he'd make a decent living without a college degree (dyslexia made school excruciatingly frustrating). He wasn't going to be an "Uncle Irving," the guy who leeches off of everyone in the family. Until he'd met Maggie, he was content to live on what he earned as an audio technician. He could wire a dozen mics in half an hour and deliver audio so clean it whistled. Phil Scott, one of the best videographers in town, had anointed him his soundman. He would never make as much money as his dad or the lobbyists, lawyers, and businesspeople who peopled Bertrand Court, but he took pride in his work.

He bought Maggie warm chocolate chip cookies from Mrs. Fields, then meandered down to Sears and picked out a modest rear-bagging job for $279.98.

When Eric returned home, Maggie was covered in spit-up. "He hasn't stopped fussing since you left."

Alec was arching his back and flailing his arms. Eric held the baby's little chest in his hand and patted him on the back, the way he'd seen his sister do once with his niece Goldie. The baby let out three enormous burps.

Maggie looked at him wide-eyed. "How did you know how to do that?"

"Hannah showed me."

Her eyes started to well up. "Christ, Eric, you've got to take your cell phone with you. You have a kid," she reprimanded him, but in a grateful, almost loving voice.

Eric handed her the nursing pads. "These are the most absorbent brand on the market."

Maggie laughed.

"I brought you cookies."

"So much for getting my figure back."

She rested her head on Eric's shoulder. He felt better now, like they'd recovered a semblance of their old selves, the unlikely match whose love would conquer all. He turned on the TV and rubbed Maggie's neck while she fed the baby and they watched reruns of *I Love Lucy*, disregarding Hannah's advice to take turns sleeping.

Maggie sat in the backseat of the car with Alec during the three-mile drive to Hannah and Danny's enormous house with a wraparound porch that had been featured in *Wash-ingtonian Magazine*. Realtor Danny had a gift for scouting out houses, or "killer screaming investment deals," as he would say through his hundred-watt smile.

Hazy sunlight streamed through the trees that fortressed the living room windows, and Brenda had filled the house with bouquets of light-blue balloons inscribed with "Welcome to the world, Alec!" She'd covered rented tables with "It's a Boy!" cloths and garnished bakery platters with fake chocolate cigars with Alec's name penned in pale blue icing. (This was tame compared to Eric's Beatles-themed bar mitzvah, complete with Ringo, John, Paul, and George centerpieces.)

Hannah had purchased the items on the mohel's list: a tube of Neosporin, Vaseline, and gauze pads. Eric tried to listen as Rabbi Katzen explained how to care for Alec's penis, but a familiar electricity filled the air, the kind that would invade his gut if he showed up at a shoot that had imploded or a gig where his band sounded like ass.

After Rabbi Katzen finished, Eric stood still and listened to the din of voices in his sister's living room: his mom asking Maggie's parents how they'd enjoyed their night in Amy's apartment; Maggie cheerfully explaining the significance of the bris to her running partner; Phil predictably hitting on Amy, who leaned into him while opening the ceremonial bottle of Manischewitz. Amy's laugh, hyenaesque and normally infectious, was like an ice pick in his eardrum. Maggie's father's kippah slid down to cover half his boxy forehead.

Rabbi Katzen shushed the room in his New Jersey baritone. "People, welcome. We're here today to name the son of

Margaret Stramm and Evan Solonsky."

Eric, too polite to hang up on a telemarketer, debated for a second whether to correct the rabbi. This was a naming, for Christ's sake, Katzen had to get it right. "It's Eric," he whispered into the rabbi's ear.

"Eric." Rabbi Katzen placed his hand over his heart and smiled. "He looks like my own Evan, a good-looking guy, this one. Forgive me." Muffled laughter filled the room as he patted Eric's cheek. "Today we'll perform a ritual that binds us as Jewish people."

Eric heard these words through the Stramms' ears. He was beginning to feel dizzy, so he took a deep breath, as he instructed nervous interviewees to do while he was fiddling with their mics. It didn't work. Alec began whimpering in Maggie's arms just as the rabbi was explaining how they would swaddle him in Grandpa Hyman's prayer shawl.

Maggie swayed from side to side, trying to calm the baby as his whimpers turned into cries. Her neck sprouted red blotches.

"Precocious boy, he knows what's coming," Rabbi Katzen joked.

Now Alec was wailing rhythmically, like an ambulance siren.

Maggie's blotches migrated to her cheeks. She leaned over to the rabbi and muttered, "I'm afraid we're going to need you to excuse us."

" Give him to me." Rabbi Katzen held out his arms.

Alec was screaming even louder now, and Maggie looked relieved to hand him over to someone who had more experience with babies. Rabbi Katzen bounced the baby up and down, and he stopped crying. Soft, relieved laughter filled the room. "What can I say? I do this every day."

Again Alec's body tensed, and the wailing resumed.

"We're really going to need a second to regroup," Maggie said firmly, pointing to the den. She grabbed Eric's arm, and they followed the rabbi out of the living room.

In the den, Rabbi Katzen turned and thrust Alec at Maggie. "What's his krotz?" he asked her accusingly.

Maggie just blinked.

"Krotz, problem. Does he have to make?"

"She just changed him. I saw her," Eric said as if he were swearing to his dad that he'd done his math homework.

"Is he hungry?"

"He already ate."

"This is what he did last night while you were out, Eric. Look at his body when he cries. He's in so much pain." Maggie looked like she was about to cry.

"Maybe it's gas." Hannah, who moved soundlessly, like a dancer or a cat, was standing in the doorway holding Goldie, while a helpless Amy hovered behind her. "That's what this one did when I ate something she didn't like."

Eric and Maggie stared at Hannah, Amy, and Helene, who was standing behind the Solonsky sisters looking worried.

"Garlic always set her off. Chocolate was bad, too," Hannah said.

Eric couldn't bring himself to meet Maggie's eyes. Drunken noodles. Mrs. Fields. Shit.

"What if he doesn't calm down?" Eric asked.

"I've never left a bris without a foreskin," Rabbi Katzen said wryly.

Maggie sat down in an armchair and stuck Alec on her breast, but he was too fussy to nurse. Helene walked over to Maggie and put out her hands to hold Alec, who nuzzled his fuzzy head against the collar of her blouse. Babies adored Helene. She rocked him back and forth until he started to doze, grudgingly handing him to Eric's father, who would hold the baby during the circumcision according to custom. Simon rested Alec on a pillow on his lap and stroked his forehead. Rabbi Katzen moved through the ceremony with incredible speed, barely taking a breath between each blessing.

For a surgeon, Simon looked pretty green, which only made Eric more nervous. Alec was whimpering again and thrashing his tiny legs. Simon began humming a Yiddish melody that Eric recognized only vaguely, yet it claimed him. Simon held Alec's ankles, just as Great-Grandpa David had held Simon's and Grandpa Hyman had held Eric's, and on and on. This felt right. His father tightened his grip as the rabbi took a scalpel and a pacifier out of his pouch.

"Okay, Eric, put this in his mouth. He'll just cry for a few seconds."

Eric parted Alec's lips and inserted the pacifier, studying the curves of his baby's ears so he wouldn't have to think too hard about what Rabbi Katzen was about to do to his penis. And then it happened, so fast and so very slowly.

The actual cutting took less than a minute, and then the rabbi, brow furrowed in the shape of a W, cleaned Alec's penis, dressed it in gauze, fastened his diaper, and swaddled him tightly.

Alec made a liar out of Rabbi Katzen; he did not stop cry-ing after a few seconds. Or a few minutes. His face turned the color of a pomegranate; his screams grew louder and louder, and his flailing limbs strained against the taut fabric of the baby blanket.

A thin line of sweat formed on Rabbi Katzen's upper lip. "He's fine, he's fine," he assured Eric.

Maggie snatched Alec from the rabbi's arms. "Then why is he screaming his head off? And why are you sweating?" she hissed, abandoning her diversity-training voice. "And why did we put him through this barbaric thing?"

The house went quiet. Not one of the thirty-plus guests made a peep. Eric's mother slipped out of the den, and he heard her say, "Please excuse us for a second, everyone. We've got a fussy little boy. Go ahead and eat. Enjoy. Make up for yes-terday!" People resumed their conversations, but in hushed tones.

"Can you try to nurse him, Maggie?" Rabbi Katzen's voice had lost its authority.

Maggie unwrapped Alec and tossed Grandpa Hyman's tal-lis they'd used during the ceremony absently onto the carpet. Eric had never seen a tallis anywhere but draped over some-one's shoulders or neatly folded inside a velvet case.

Rabbi Katzen picked up the tallis and handed it to Eric. "The procedure went fine. He'll be fine."

Eric just nodded.

"I'll give you some privacy, but I won't leave the house un-til he's calm." The rabbi exited the den.

Alec alternately nursed and cried into Maggie's bare breast while she caressed his head, a strand of hair escaping from her barrette, brushing against her nose. An hour before, Eric would have tucked it behind her ear.

When they got home, Maggie whisked Alec away to his room. Eric sat outside the nursery and rested his head against the cool plaster of the doorway. He listened to the baby glider click as it moved back and forth above the hardwood floor. He thought about the days that would follow. He would snap more photos of Alec and eat more casseroles and watch more infomercials while he rocked the baby back to sleep in the middle of the night. He would fast next Yom Kippur, not for his father or to prove anything to Maggie, but for Alec — and for himself. He would not deny Maggie Alec's baptism, he would hide painted eggs in the backyard, he would never point out that not once since he'd known his wife had she uttered the name Jesus or stepped foot in a church, not on Easter Sunday or Christmas Eve. A bris for a baptism. A transaction sealed with blood and water.

When he could no longer hear the glider, he peeked into Alec's room. Maggie didn't open her eyes as he lifted his little boy from her shoulder. He held Alec's warm body against his, breathing in the scent of breast milk and Neutrogena soap. He changed Alec's bandages; his penis looked like a piece of raw meat.

Alec could barely keep his eyes open, so Eric put him in his bassinet and went outside to assemble his new lawn

mower. Still wearing his dress khakis and a sweat-stained but-
ton-down shirt Maggie had placed under their Christmas tree
last December, he mowed every blade of grass surrounding
the house. When he finished, he stood on his lawn as he had
the day before, but he wasn't waiting. He wasn't waiting for
Maggie to wake up, or for the fading sun to mark the end of a
long day, or for his father to notice his grass, green from a wet
September and perfectly cut.

YOU'RE NEXT

Helene Stramm and Maggie Stramm Solonsky, August 2001

I keep mum when my daughter, Maggie, tells me that she's baking a sugar-free birthday cake for my five-year-old granddaughter. It's too easy to ruffle her feathers, and I don't want to muck up our weekend together. During the drive to the health food store in Bethesda, I tolerate her "I can't believe you smoked while you were pregnant" tone while she lectures me on how sweets wreak havoc on the immune system.

My Pic 'n Save back home looks pretty gosh-darned good compared to this dump. I bite my tongue instead of asking Maggie why organic produce looks so mangy, or if all the employees are required to pierce their nostrils, or why she chooses to shop in a store that smells like a scented bathroom candle. Little Kaya and I follow her up and down the aisles in search of some magical artificial sweetener her acupuncturist recommended.

"Found it." Maggie reaches for a rectangular box decorated with a drawing of a mint leaf. "This is it, Say-Lo. I remember the name because it sounds like J. Lo."

"The Italian singer with the round derrière?"

"She's Puerto Rican, Mom." Maggie laughs, and then Kaya and I join in. The joke's on me, and that's okay, as long as we're all laughing together.

A bearded clerk gives Maggie the once-over while he rings up the Say-Lo. And why not? My Maggie's pretty again, in a bohemian kind of way. She doesn't have to resort to the bottle (L'Oréal No. 12) like I did once I hit my mid-thirties. A natural honey color tints her long braid, and she keeps herself real slim and trim. Thank the good Lord, she's over the phase where she dyed her hair black and ate junk and made herself as unappealing as possible. This was right before she flitted off to London, and we didn't speak for a year. But then one day out of the blue, she called to tell me that she was getting married. Eric's a Jewish fellow, which took a little getting used to, odd customs and all. It's true what they say about the Jewish people though, they certainly know the meaning of family, and Eric's been good for her.

The clerk gestures to us. "No question you three apples fell from the same tree." He points his index finger at me but looks at Kaya. "Now, is this your mom's twin sister?" With that twinkle in his eyes, he's starting to remind me of a scruffy Cary Grant.

"She's my grandma, silly." Kaya giggles and points to my ash-blond hair (L'Oréal No. 30).

I cup her cheek, the perfect half of a peach, and gush, "You're very kind, young man." Good golly, it's been a long while since anyone's noticed my looks. But here I am, the source of both Maggie's and Kaya's dimples and light hair, a sharp contrast to our olive skin. A striking combination, if I do say so myself. Now, Kaya's older brother Alec is all Solonsky — dark hair, doughy body, and gentle eyes, albeit a little too close together. Real Jewish-looking, like his father.

Kaya waves goodbye to the clerk, and I reach for her hand as we exit the store. I squeeze her chubby fingers, which will one day be long and tapered like mine. It's hot outside, and the humidity is downright uncivilized for a Midwestern girl like me. I take a handkerchief out of my pocketbook and dab my upper lip.

"Doesn't that clerk remind you of Cary Grant a little?" I ask Maggie.

She rolls her eyes. "He's a big flirt."

"What's a flirt?" Kaya asks as she hops into the back of Maggie's wagon and buckles her car seat.

"A person who makes people feel good about themselves so they'll like him," Maggie says, starting the car.

"People are going to flirt with you like crazy, Kaya. You're such a pretty little thing." I smile at her in the rearview mirror.

Maggie's jaw tenses. She's so fussy about this topic. Can't I appreciate my granddaughter's beauty?

"Kaya and I have big discussions about *inner* beauty, about the importance of kindness and respect." Maggie's doing that thing she does with her husband, where they pretend that they're talking to each other: "Kaya cleaned up her room today, Eric. All by herself." But this time I can't tell if her intended audience is Kaya or me.

"And inclusion, Mommy. That means you let everyone play with you." Kaya has rehearsed this line.

"That's right, sweetie." Maggie shoots me a look, the remnants of a familiar anger that I still don't understand. I never worked so hard at anything in my life as I did raising my daughter, devoting myself to her, helping her strive for perfection. If my mother had paid attention to me like that when I was a girl, I would have luxuriated in her love like a kitten basking in a warm patch of sunshine. I thought when Maggie became a mother she would understand the sacrifices I made for her, the hours I spent learning her cheerleading routine so I could help her make the squad. Which she did.

But I'm not going to let any of that spoil my weekend. You could have knocked me over with a feather when Maggie called last month and asked me to fly to Washington to help out with Kaya's party. Sure, we see each other fairly often — Christmas, birthdays, and whatnot — but this is the first time she's really invited me into her life since Alec's circumcision ceremony, the first time she hasn't pawned me off on her kooky sister-in-law Amy, who lives in a cute little apartment in a Spanish neighborhood near the zoo. Amy insists that the neighborhood is safe, but I send her bottles of mace from time to time. Eric and Alec are off at some father-son soccer camp in Pennsylvania — neither one has an athletic bone in his body, something I'd never dare mention. So here I am, ready to roll up my sleeves.

———

My mother thinks that baking a sugar-free carrot cake for a five-year-old's birthday party is moronic, as she's been screaming at me by her deliberate silences since I took her to the Bethesda Natural Food Co-op this afternoon. I'm not going to let it get to me; our parenting styles are just completely opposite — thank God — and she's going to have to accept that eliminating sugar from our diet is an important choice I'm making for our family.

I prepare a farro and cilantro dish I clipped from *Organic Weekly*, steam some kale, and broil a nice piece of salmon for us. After dinner, I bathe Kaya, whose little body hums with excitement over the party; it takes three chapters of *Charlotte's Web* for her to drift off to sleep.

My mother is scouring the salmon pan with an S.O.S. pad when I join her in the kitchen. "Thank goodness she finally went down. I don't want her to be pooped out for her party," she says, and she smiles at me, which incites a fresh wave of guilt over my anger with her this afternoon at the co-op. I ruined her moment with Stephen, or the Compliment Man, as Eric and I've nicknamed him. I pick up a bag of carrots, and we grate them until our fingers turn orange.

"Look." I point to our stained hands.

"That's carotene." She rubs her fingers together. "Your father loved carrots. Remember that ginger-carrot ring I used to serve on Christmas Eve?" Her voice softens, as it always does when she remembers my father, who died last summer.

"Yes, and I remember our baking adventures too."

My mother's the most fun when she's baking. We used to make batches of M&M oatmeal cookies to sell at high school football games when I cheered, and I bet if I put on some Captain & Tennille she'd start dancing, despite her recent hip replacement.

Maybe Eric's idea of inviting her to help with Kaya's party wasn't so bad. "Birthday parties are Helene's thing, Maggie. Besides, she's so lonely without your dad," he said last month as we drove home from picking strawberries. Things are much better with my mom; I mean, I don't hate her anymore. She was so invested in my looks that I felt like she was breathing through my lungs. Now that I'm a mom myself, I can't imagine taking that kind of pleasure in my daughter's appearance. I want to show my mother that raising children is about instilling values and building self-esteem, not pushing them so hard to be on top of the heap that they grow fat, pimply, and miserable out of spite. I can't imagine what it would take for her to get that.

I invited both of Eric's sisters to the party, and the next morning Hannah and her younger daughter, Jane, arrive at ten-thirty on the nose. I also invited Robin and Sydney, but they're in Rochester visiting Marcus's family.

Kaya bounces downstairs wearing her favorite pair of overalls and a dingy Snow White T-shirt Eric bought her at the Orlando airport two years ago. My mother examines Kaya, and I know she's thinking, *Couldn't she have put on a party dress?* When Kaya learned how to dress herself, I made a silent promise that I would let her choose her own clothes, regardless of how unattractive they were.

Thank God, Hannah brought Jane, because only six children show up for the party. Two of them are twin girls from across the street. I've tried to befriend their mother, Nikki, but

she's aloof. Their father, Tad, walks them over, and I can practically hear my mother wishing I'd married a man like him, the
kind who wears expensive suits, whitens his teeth, and greets
you with both polite attention and the suggestion that someone or someplace more important awaits him. A son-in-law
her cronies at the club would covet. Tad's the polar opposite
of Eric, not my type, but I do wish he'd stay, just to fill out the
room.

"August is a tough month to host anything in Washington.
The city just clears out," Hannah explains to my mother, and I
resent her kindness.

My mother's eyes dart around the room. "Go get me one
of your scarves, Maggie, and I'll lead the girls in a game of Pin
the Tail on the Donkey."

"This is a choose-your-own-theme birthday party, Mom."
I try to keep the annoyance out of my voice. I've explained this
to her about a dozen times, but she refuses to hear me. "It's
empowering for the girls to make this experience what they
want it to be for themselves."

As per usual, Amy, whom Kaya has deemed "the fun aunt,"
arrives late. She sneaks Kaya a kiss and heads to the sunroom
to join my mother and Hannah, who are rocking back and
forth in their wicker chairs. They pepper Amy with questions
about her boyfriend, Leon. None of us have met him yet. I notice that Hannah keeps a watchful eye on the kids, the way I
did when my sweet, pudgy Alec was playing T-ball with a team
of rough boys.

As I'm putting the finishing touches on the goodie bags in
the kitchen, my attention slides toward the living room, where

I can see Kaya's reflection in the glass cabinet.

She stands with her hands on her hips and points to Jane and two other girls. "You three go draw, and when I say time's up, then Sophie and Emma will switch and two of you can come play house with me," she orders. "I'll decide which two." During a parent conference last winter, her teacher had described this bossy behavior, which I initially chalked up to her classmate Daphne Silverberg's bad influence. After Daphne moved to Toronto, I attributed the bossiness to Kaya's burgeoning leadership abilities.

The three girls dutifully march off to color on a small table, and Kaya turns her attention to Sophie and Emma, the anointed guests. "Okay, so I'm the mommy. Emma, you're the daddy."

Emma grins.

"What am I?" Sophie asks.

Kaya pauses as Sophie waits in silence. "You're their dog. And you have bad breath."

Sophie's shoulders slump, and her chin quivers.

"Here, put this in your mouth." Kaya gives her a ratty old tennis ball she must have found in the yard.

Emma giggles nervously and doesn't stick up for her twin sister.

"In your mouth, Sophie," Kaya says sweetly.

It feels like red heat is smoking off my chest. I hope to God that Hannah, Amy, and my mother are so deep in conversation, now about mace, that they're not catching this. Should I step in? Reprimand Kaya on her birthday? Tell Sophie not to put the ball in her mouth? I wish Eric were here, even though he rarely takes on his little princess, or his big princess either, come to think of it.

"You're next, Emma. Go get the tennis ball." Kaya hugs her redheaded friend.

Emma purrs at Kaya's affection and picks up the ball. Holy shit, my daughter is cult leader material.

Jane, shy yet self-assured, has dealt herself out of this game; she's looking through a stack of Kaya's puzzles in the corner of the den. I feign oblivion to the goings-on in the sunroom. "So, Hannah, did you tell my mom about your trip to the Dells?" I try to drown Kaya out, because I'm hearing her through their ears. This is a train wreck. But something about Kaya's control over these little girls tugs at the borders of my consciousness. Although I'm not exactly proud of her behavior, I'm a little in awe of her power.

"Girls, time to serve the cake!" I finally interrupt Kaya's game.

The girls gather around a card table my mother has decorated with pink balloons and streamers. My mother places the round layer cake in front of Kaya while I hunt down our camera. A halo of candlelight bathes Kaya's face and hair, and she's my angel again. I snap a shot of her blowing out all five candles on the first try. My mother plucks out the slender candles, covered in a gummy orange substance and white frosting. The cake's a big hit, and when Sophie asks for seconds, my mother nods at me with approval. I've spent the better part of my life pissed off at her, but right now I feel prouder than the day I ran home breathless with the news that I'd been voted captain of the cheerleading squad.

———

Kaya "whoopses" the first time during her birthday bounce on Robin and Marcus's trampoline, a few hours after the guests have all gone home. Thank goodness the Golds are in Rochester and were therefore spared the sight of an orange geyser flying into the blue sky. Maggie and I chalk it up to the heat, the excitement, and too much activity on a full tummy. Then the cake comes out both ends while Maggie is bathing Kaya, and again when the poor little dear stretches out on her Sleeping Beauty bedspread. We assume she's finished when we bring her down to the sunroom to cuddle and listen to the rest of *Charlotte's Web*, but she gets sick all over the wicker chair, ruining the page where Charlotte spells her first word. Maggie carries her to the bathroom, but only after Kaya has managed to make quite a mess of the sunroom, which looks like orange you-know-what really did hit a fan. I'm guessing Kaya snitched another piece of cake before dinner. There is nothing worse than the sound of a child retching. I run down to the corner market and buy some Gatorade and good old-fashioned Coca-Cola, like I used to give Maggie whenever she got sick.

When I return, Maggie has opened the windows to ventilate the sunroom. The thick air carries the scent of bleach and Say-Lo, which smells like burnt rubber. Maggie would have been better off baking a less colorful cake.

"Hand me that 409, dear. I'll wipe down this chair," I offer after Kaya has finally fallen asleep.

Maggie doesn't answer me because the phone rings. I begin to dig into the weave of the wicker chair, trying not to breathe in too deeply. Her voice is full of apology as she talks to Tad's wife, Nikki, the twins' mother. "I spoke with Poison Control already. It's not toxic in the quantity I used for the cake."

She hangs up and sweeps her wet hair off her neck. "Don't, Mom. I know what you're thinking," she says through the hair band she's holding in her teeth.

"I'm not saying a word."

"You're thinking why didn't I just buy one of those sheet cakes from the Giant, all lard and sugar, with princesses and mounds of pink and purple frosting?"

That's exactly what I'm thinking, but I've done a very good job of keeping quiet, and I'm sure not going to throw kerosene on this fire. I'm also thinking that Maggie could easily have married somebody like Nikki's Tad, but that's not productive either. "Actually, I was thinking about what marvelous self-esteem Kaya has developed. She has quite a Svengali effect on those little girls." No big surprise, she's smart and gorgeous, but if I mention her looks, Maggie will flip into one of her moods. Pretty is bad. Confident is good. Got it.

Maggie answers the phone again. "Hi, Amy." She shifts feet.

This isn't going to be good. Amy ate the frosting off of everyone's plate. I saw her do it. Such an odd woman, that Amy.

"I know. Wait, that's my call waiting. I'm so sorry. God, this is a disaster." Maggie pushes down on the receiver and answers the next call. "How many times?" she asks, then gives her Poison Control spiel and hangs up. "Megan Moore. Her

Aliza ate a lot of cake."

"Oh, dear," I say.

"I better call Hannah," Maggie says. She's nervous; her chest is breaking out in those red blotches. Maybe she'll feel better if we talk about our dazzling Kaya some more. "Your daughter was cuing those girls like a director when they played with those tiny dolls. Polly Pockets, I think she called them? Cute. And she assigned two mommies to one child!"

Maggie removes a soiled slipcover from one of the couch pillows. "Kaya has a lot of classmates in her preschool with same-sex parents."

Oh, Lord have mercy, she's going to hop on that diversity soapbox with that hideous tone she uses to lecture all of us who "don't get it." I've never figured out exactly what it is that I don't get, or why people who do get it are so gosh-darned mean to those who don't. That girl can make me mad as a hornet. I muster up a smile and reach for another roll of paper towels. My, it feels like a sauna in here. My blouse sticks to the dampness under my arms.

Maggie continues in that tone of hers. "So the preschool furnishes some of the dramatic play areas with only mommy dolls and others with daddy dolls."

I wasn't going to say anything about the tennis ball incident, but it's always like this with Maggie. I'm her punching bag. "Kaya was pretty tough on that cute little Sophie, told her that she had to be the dog when they played house." I give the chair another good squirt of cleaner.

Maggie's ears turn crimson. "Eric and I appreciate the diversity in her preschool. We want Kaya to know that everyone, regardless of his or her sexual preference or race or religion, should be loved and accepted for who they are." She's heaping naked pillows on top of one another.

"And when Sophie started to cry, Kaya went in for the kill." I lower my voice, knowing that my calm is just going to make her hotter. I gave birth to this girl, taught her her first word, and bought her her first brassiere; I know where she hides the silver.

Maggie ignores my comment. "These are our core values."

Oh, for Pete's sake, if I hear one more word about their "values," I might just have to wait in line behind Kaya for the toilet. "Your daughter runs the show. She's got the others lining up for her approval."

"Kaya has not yet learned the social skills to manage all the girls who vie for her attention. It's a developmental issue." Maggie's voice is loud.

Hooey. I'm about to tell Maggie she can move to London or Timbuktu and I'm still her mother and I can still read her and her little girl like a Harlequin. I saw everything. Kaya will always land on top of the heap, despite Maggie's mumbo jumbo about equality. And I'll tell little Miss We Treat Everyone with Respect that I watched her watch Kaya take charge of those little girls and I caught a smile poke through her lips. She can't deny how delicious it feels to see your child win.

Before I can say any of this, the phone rings again, and Maggie looks at the caller ID. "This is a nightmare," she says in a tone of dread. "Hi, Hannah. I was just going to call you." She pauses. "Oh, that's such a sweet thing to say." Now she sounds almost chipper. "I'd love to chat, but we're just putting our house back together. Thanks for calling." Maggie grins. "Jane must not have eaten the cake!"

I can't tell if Maggie's happy that her niece didn't get sick or that someone actually called to compliment her on the party, especially Hannah. She looks like she did when she used to do those tap routines for my mother, eager to please, vulnerable to my mother's boozy indifference — and Maggie was the favorite grandchild. I wanted to mess up my mother's Greta Garbo hairdo, scoop my little girl up in my arms, and cover her with kisses.

The anger vacates my body, and now I'm just dog-tired. And sad. Why do Maggie and I fight when she needs me the most? My limbs feel heavy, and my eyes burn. I want to hug my daughter, but I can't face her turning away from me again.

"Remember when I hired the Mary Kay lady to make up all our faces at your sweet sixteen?"

Maggie nods her head. "Who knew that poor Rhonda Anderson would break out in such a rash? What was that chemical she was allergic to?"

"One of the dyes in the blusher, I think." Methylparaben, I'll never forget that one. "See, dear, I'm not so old that I can't remember what it's like to ruin a child's birthday party." I offer this as an olive branch, but Maggie's laughter trails off. The only sound in the room is my paper towel digging into the soiled wicker chair.

———

Fuck Eric. He should be here right now phoning the remaining guests and helping me clean this mess up, and then my mother wouldn't be comforting me for ruining Kaya's birthday party. Stupid, stupid, stupid. I should have researched the side effects of that damned sweetener. What kind of acupuncturist smokes, anyway? I wish my mother would just go upstairs and take a bath or something, but there's a part of me that wants her to stay. Story of my life.

We use two rolls of paper towels to clean the chair. Much to my surprise, it actually feels good to wipe away the mess with her. When I was a little girl and I was worried about a test or remembering my lines for a school play, I would lie in bed and wait for my mother to come sit on the edge and stroke my forehead. Just like that, my worries would dissolve, like the graphite designs on Kaya's Etch A Sketch when you shake it. Presto. Gone. The sheer act of the telling made them disappear. Okay, here goes nothing.

"Kaya makes her friends tell her secrets if they want to play with her. Sophie told Kaya that another girl's mother — a pediatrician, no less — makes her eat off the floor. 'Germs on her terms,' her mother calls it, something about immunity boosting. Kaya told everyone during circle time, and the little girl was so embarrassed that she cried for the rest of the day." I deliver my confession in one breath.

"Did Kaya invite the girl to the party?" My mother's tone is soft.

"What do you think?" I almost laugh, but I can feel tears creeping up behind my eyeballs. "No wonder the other mothers quit the Mean Girls, Zero Tolerance Task Force as soon as I joined."

"Mags, maybe it wasn't because of you." Her voice softens

further.

For a second my shoulders relax, and then the tension returns with a snapping sensation. "Most of the mothers hate
me."

"Hannah and Amy don't."

"Mom, Amy isn't a mom, and did you see the way Hannah
was hawking over the girls?" I wish my voice wasn't shaking.

"What do the other moms say, darling?"

"They say I can't see how manipulative Kaya is, that I en-
courage it because I'm proud of her power."

"Are you?"

"No," I answer too quickly.

She lets my half-truth go. "How do you know this?" she
asks.

"I overheard a couple of mothers talking at the school
auction. Only a few of the ten girls we invited to Kaya's party
came, and two of them were neighbors."

My mother puts down her sponge, and for the second
time tonight she moves toward me, and I wonder again if she's
going to gather me up in her arms and hold me. She pauses
and then sits down.

"They hated me too," she says. Now she looks like a rum-
pled little girl, slumped in a corner of the sunroom, with a wad
of dirty paper towels in her hand. Years of tanning have leath-
ered her skin, a tiny pouch hangs over the waistband of her
pink Lilly Pulitzer capris, and her arms look bony, loose skin
puckering at the elbows. I want to tell her that it's okay, that
every call she made to the school, every diet she put me on,
every backseat coaching session she gave me, she did because

she loved me, in her way. I forgive her for making me practice my cheers in the driveway until my fingers turned numb from the Wisconsin autumn cold and relentlessly comparing my looks to the other girls'. I forgive the stony silences on the way home from running errands, after the butcher smiled at me while she batted her eyelashes. Did I choose to get fat and dye my hair because I wanted her to back off, or because I wanted the butchers and mailmen and electricians to flirt with her and not me? Or both?

I want one of those double-hanky moments portrayed on the family television dramas I used to watch as a child, where everyone hugs and cries and then trots off to the kitchen to scoop out big bowls of ice cream with hot fudge sauce. But my kitchen still smells like Say-Lo, an aroma I will forever link to vomit and humiliation. And my mother does not bring out my inner compassionate TV drama daughter; I am stuck as the petulant teenager who ran from her like hell. Instead of hugging her, I speak a truth, because right now that's the best I have to offer.

"I bet those mothers loved it when I went through my little rebellion."

Without a beat she returns my lob. "Why do you think I stopped shopping at Food Lane? You were the talk of the checkout line." The depth of the shame I caused her exposes itself to me, and for the first time in my life, I can actually see her as someone other than the person who makes me crazy.

She points to the baseboard and sprays 409 on a fossilized boxelder bug, snow-boot scuff marks, and a crooked line of blue crayon. We kneel before this shrine of daily life and pick up our sponges. The detergent has cleansed the orange tint from our skin, returning it to its natural color, perhaps a little pinker and puffy from the heat. We share the same tapered fingers and small, unattractive nail beds that manicures only magnify. An age spot the shape of an egg sprouts between my mother's first two knuckles. Otherwise, our hands are identical as we scrub old stains.

IN FLIGHT

Rosie Gold, April 2002

When Marcus picks Mom and me up from the airport — we've flown in from Rochester for our annual cherry blossom visit — he does that thing where he looks at you and past you at the same time. He doesn't think I notice because I'm his crazy big sister, a little slow, a little off. I lost too much oxygen at birth. People always want to label me "tard" or PDD or high-functioning this or that, but I'm just Rosie. Rosie Gold.

"Can you give me some air back here?" When Robin drives me, she knows to point the vents toward the backseat, but she's not here.

"She's still going through the change," Mom informs Marcus in a hushed voice. "Menopause."

"Privacy, Mom!" Does she think I'm deaf?

"Speaking of privacy, they made me take my shoes off at the airport!"

"Security is tight since 9/11, Mom," Marcus says.

"Lucky we wore clean socks, right Rosie?" Mom calls over her shoulder.

Mom can be funny sometimes. "Sure are, Mom."

Mom focuses her attention back on Marcus. "So did the kids go gaga over their new cousin?"

A couple of days ago, Robin took their kids to Memphis to see her sister's new baby, but they flew back this morning, and they must be home waiting for us. I can't wait; they haven't visited us in ninety-seven days, and I haven't seen Sydney do her new moves on the trampoline, even though they bought it last July when Sydney started getting serious about gymnastics.

Marcus turns onto his street, the cherry blossom trees in full bloom.

"The Enchanted Bertrand Forest." I remind everyone of Dad's nickname for Marcus's neighborhood.

"Gorgeous." Mom agrees and then pats her middle. "I didn't eat a thing this morning. Travel nerves, you know." She sighs. Dad used to hold Mom's hand when we flew, but he died two years ago. "We'll have a nosh with Robin and the kids."

"Mom," Marcus blurts, "I didn't know how to tell you this, but Robin called. Justin has an ear infection. He's fine, but he can't fly until some of the fluid dries up."

"But they'll come home tomorrow, right, Marcus?"

Mom gives me the look to lower my voice, which she thinks gets loud when I'm upset, which I am. Everyone's seen Sydney's braces but me, and I want to talk to Justin about his bar mitzvah. It's not for a year, but I want to tell him that he should have an ice cream sundae bar. Marcus told me that Justin calls me his special Aunt Rosie. That made me feel good because he means special in a good way.

Marcus pulls into the driveway, takes the keys out of the

ignition, and says over his shoulder, "You'll see them tomorrow, Rosie. Promise."

"God willing," Mom adds.

God willing is right.

It's warm outside, and all of the neighbors have pulled out
their Adirondack chairs — blues and purples and greens — for
the spring and summer. We stand in Marcus's driveway and
Mom closes her eyes and tilts her head toward the sun. She's
got liver spots on her cheeks. We have the same kind of skin,
dark and dry around the nose, so I'll probably get marks like
those one day, too.

Mom smiles up at the bright blue sky. "You should never
know from the winter we had."

"Ordered the weather just for you two." Marcus kisses her
hair, so full of spray that it covers her head like a helmet.

We barely get a spring in Rochester. What's that joke? We
have two seasons, July and winter. I don't get it, but it seems
like it should be funny, so I always laugh when people tell it.

We walk around to the backyard, to Marcus's trampoline.
Mom stares at it with this funny look in her eyes. I figure she's
going to tell us the story about Joey Hellman, our neighbor
who broke his back doing a double flip on his trampoline. She
always tells us this story when she sees Marcus's trampoline,
but this time she doesn't.

Inside, the house doesn't smell of its usual sugar and butter. Robin's always baking something, which I think is weird
because Marcus owns a bakery. "It's not that kind of bakery,"

he tells me. "We're wholesalers. We only distribute bread." What kind of bakery doesn't bake cookies?

I follow Marcus to the basement. He puts my suitcase in the guest room and stands there for an extra few seconds, almost as if he's waiting for Justin or Sydney to do something cute for us to laugh at, or for Robin to holler downstairs to remind him to put the clothes in the dryer, or for his bakery to call him on his cell phone.

He turns on Nickelodeon. Greg, Peter, and Bobby Brady are kicking the girls out of their clubhouse. I haven't watched this episode of *The Brady Bunch* since Justin was born, but I remember wishing that Marcus and I would fight, and then to make up with me, he'd build a clubhouse for us to share. I sit on the edge of the sleeper sofa real straight so I won't muss up my travel dress. After another episode, I go upstairs where Marcus is setting the table.

"That Robin. Look." Mom points to the counter and the frozen packages with "Cherry Blossom Visit" written on Post-it notes taped to the foil.

Mom heats the food in the microwave and then motions us to sit down. "I've been listening to the local news. They're predicting a nor'easter," Mom warns.

I don't like this talk of snow.

Mom waves her hand and chuckles. "A few inches and you'll close your schools for a good week, and the grocery stores will run out of toilet paper."

"Does this mean that Justin won't be able to show me his new skateboard?" The snow will ruin everything. "We'll all be stuck in the house forever," I add grumpily.

"We've had so many false alarms this year," Marcus reassures us, trying not to seem nervous, but he is, and it's making me nervous too, and I'm not sure what we're so nervous about. "Spring is here to stay." He nods to the kitchen window, and we all look out at the long rows of cherry blossoms against the blue and orange sky.

Mom raises her second glass of wine to her lips and points to the trampoline. "You know, that brings back a lot of memories."

I'm still waiting for the Joey Hellman story, but she surprises me with a new one.

"When you were three and a half, Rosie, and you were just two months old, Marcus, your father and I were invited to the Bloomsteins' house on Canandaigua Lake for a barbecue."

I butt in. "Did you bring us?" I hate it when people leave me out.

"God, no. This was an adult party. Quite wet, if you know what I mean."

"Wet?" Marcus asks.

"We enjoyed our cocktails. I wore a lavender shirtwaist with yellow daisies embroidered on the collar." She fingers her faded black sweater. "I climbed up on their trampoline and jumped like a little bird." Mom closes her eyes and flutters her hands. "I bounced higher and higher until I was schvitzing." And then she opens her eyes suddenly, as if she's pulling herself out of a dream. "Your father shouted, 'Essie,'" — Mom's voice gets deep and loud like Dad's — "'you have a little girl and an infant at home to take care of. What are you thinking?'" She slaps her thigh, but she doesn't laugh. "I looked over at him, and he was plenty scared, your father. He could barely change a diaper, so I got off and gave Lenore Rabin a turn."

"You never told me that story," Marcus says softly.

Later that night, right before I drift off to sleep, I remember the morning before Joey Hellman broke his back. I was too scared to jump on his trampoline, so I just sat on the black cross in the middle, and Marcus bounced me high into the air until we were both laughing our heads off. He looked like a bird too.

The next morning I wake up to more snow than we even have in Rochester; the Weather Channel says nine inches and a threat of five more to follow. Robin's yellow daffodils are covered in a fat white blanket, and I can't even see the trampoline.

I slide on my slippers and poke my head into Marcus's office. "I guess the weatherman was right this time, Markie."

He pounds away at his computer, raising his forefinger in the hold-on-a-second gesture he uses with Justin when he's being a pest. "Robin and the kids won't be able to fly in today," he tells me, like it's my fault or something.

I shuffle out of his office while he talks to his bakery people in a much nicer tone than he was using with me. If the kids were here, I'd be watching television with them and wouldn't care that Mr. Big was too busy for me.

Mom's making coffee in the kitchen. "I'll fix you some eggs," she offers.

I join her in the breakfast room and sit in my usual chair, which faces the family photo taken at Marcus and Robin's wedding. I always thought that I'd marry first because I'm older, so I was a crab apple at the reception until Robin's brother Danny grabbed my hand to dance the hora.

"Remember what you told Dad at the wedding?"

"What, Rosie?" Mom says, slicing a piece of challah.

"You told him that Danny's date's bazooms were falling out of her top."

She doesn't look up from the challah. "Danny didn't hear me."

"Oh yes." I wouldn't make this up. "He did, Mom. Everybody heard you."

"Rosie, please." She purses her lips.

"I'm glad he married Hannah," I say.

Mom nods absently.

"Her bazooms are much smaller than the girl Danny brought to the wedding. Right, Mom?"

"Oh, Rosie," Mom says.

Now I've annoyed her, which is easy to do when we're traveling.

We eat our soft boiled eggs and watch the news. When Marcus finally comes out of his office, I'm standing in front of the fridge sipping my OJ.

He taps my shoulder with his finger. "Rosie, you want to come to the store with me?"

Mom frowns. "She just got over a cold. Do you really think she should be traipsing around in the wet snow?"

"That was three weeks ago. Jeez!" She treats me like I'm seven. I run downstairs to change; I'm not mad at Marcus anymore.

The cul-de-sac is sparkly white, and there's so much snow on the branches that you can barely see any pink blossoms. Two boys across the street are swatting at snowballs with baseball bats, laughing when the slush sprays them in the face. I wave at them, but they must not see me, because they keep playing with each other. That happens to me a lot.

Marcus and I split shoveling the driveway, just like we used to do in high school. He tosses a shovelful of snow at me, like those kids across the street, and I giggle when it lands on Robin's parka, which pulls around my middle because I'm plump now. This happens with middle age, Mom tells me.

After we finish, Marcus opens the van door for me. He searches for an oldies station on the radio, and we listen to the Monkees, just like we did when we used to drive to temple with Dad. I tell Marcus about Anthony, the janitor from my apartment building, who looks like a chubbier, balding version of David Cassidy. Once when he came to fix my thermostat, I offered him some ginger snaps and an ice-cold glass of milk. He accepted. Eventually, he'd ask me to the movies or for a hamburger, I figured. Now he's getting married.

Marcus fumbles for something to say. "You'll meet someone else, Rosie. Remember what Dad used to tell us? Every pot..."

"...has a lid."

"That's right." He fiddles with his cap.

"Like Ginny Rae?" When I was in high school, all the kids had to watch *Like Normal People*, a movie about Ginny Rae and Roger, a retarded couple who get married. Katie Buck and her friends started calling me Ginny Rae, which made no sense because that actress Linda Purl had blue eyes and a button nose.

"Who's Ginny Rae?" he asks. How could he not have known that's what people called me? He sat tables away from me in the cafeteria, but Katie Buck was really loud. When she started calling me and my friend Fern Ginny Raetard, I told on her and Mr. Rand, our school principal, made her write me an apology note. When my dad said that he was proud of me for sticking up for myself, Marcus left the dinner table without eating his wax beans. He loves wax beans.

"So, has Mom been on your case?" He changes the subject.

"Huh? Oh, you mean about my cold?"

"In general."

"She's just being Mom."

He turns down the radio so we can barely hear my favorite Chiffons song. "Do you think she's a little down?"

"Do *you* think she is?"

He adjusts the defroster. "Maybe a little tired?"

Dad got tired a lot before he found out about his bad heart. "Do you think Mom's sick?"

"I'm sure she's fine," he says and returns his attention to the road.

He's scaring me. "Are we going to be orphans?"

Marcus pushes the brakes too hard when he tries to stop at the light, and the car skids a little. "Rosie, the roads are slick. I better concentrate."

He drives extra carefully the rest of the way to the Giant.

"I'll take care of you, Markie. That's what big sisters do," I tell him as we're getting out of the car. He won't believe me, because he was the one who used to take care of me when we were kids. I'd huff off to my room and throw myself around, and Marcus would come and sit on my carpet, and sort his baseball cards until I calmed down. But when he got older he stayed in his own room most of the time except for when he and Dad would sit in the den drinking root beer and watching the Bills.

"That's right, Rosie. You're my big sister," he tells me over his shoulder, still without meeting my eyes.

Marcus and I wait in a twenty-minute checkout line at the Giant. He buys the last carton of milk, a three-pound canister of prunes for Mom, hot dogs for me, and half a cartful of other food all totaling seventy-three dollars and thirty-two cents. I've never spent more than thirty-one dollars at the grocery store, but then, I eat the exact same thing every day: a bowl of Life cereal with two-percent milk for breakfast, a peanut butter and strawberry jelly sandwich for lunch, and a Stouffer's manicotti for dinner.

On the way home from the grocery store, Marcus's cell phone rings.

"Hi!"

I can tell it's Robin on the line, because his whole face breaks into a grin. When he smiles at Mom and me, he only uses his mouth.

"The Giant parking lot with Rosie. How's Justin?"

"Rosie, they're coming home tomorrow morning," he says as if he's just found out the best news of his life. He used to look like this right after he'd wolfed down his dinner so he could go visit Mindy Greenblatt, his high school girlfriend.

When we get home, Marcus makes a business call while Mom puts the groceries away, rearranging Robin's pantry in the process. Mom's pouring milk in a pan for cocoa when Marcus tells us that one of his delivery trucks slid into a snow bank on the way to a hotel out in Virginia, his bakery's biggest account. The driver fractured his collarbone. "I've got to take care of this, it's a disaster. You and Rosie want to take a nap or watch something on television?"

"Maybe we'll stretch out. I had a big week." She turns to me. "We went and got our mammograms together Tuesday, I had the podiatrist Wednesday, and lunch with Muriel Kaplan on Thursday. Such a noodge, always at me to winter with her in Boynton Beach when she knows I don't have the time."

"I remember when the two of you volunteered for Planned Parenthood. You wore those necklaces with the gold-plated hangers." Marcus taps his Adam's apple and glances at the silver chain around Mom's neck. Dad's wedding band hangs there now.

"I remember those hangers, Mom." As soon as I say this, she and Marcus give each other one of those looks I hate, like I've missed something. Everyone knows what happens to a baby when you swallow a coat hanger. Please.

"Why don't you take Muriel up on her offer and spend time with her in Florida next winter? Take Rosie with you."

"I have a job, Marcus." He's getting me mad again. Does he think he's the only one with responsibilities? My boss once told me that I'm the hardest working employee the Toy Chest ever hired, and that I understand more about stuffed animals and games than he does. I huff off to my bedroom and watch back-to-back episodes of *The Facts of Life*. Robin bought me two whole seasons on DVD, and this is the one where Tudie steals a present for Mrs. Garrett because she can't afford to buy one herself. Tudie is my favorite character.

On my way to the bathroom, I notice the door to the second guest room is open a crack. Mom's curled into a ball on the edge of the bed. She never used to nap. I shut the door and rush back to my room just in time to catch Mrs. Garrett making one of her funny faces. That makes me feel better.

"I'm sorry if I made you mad," Marcus says as he appears in my doorway. "I just worry about you and Mom."

"If you worry so much, why don't you ever call?" I feel like I'm going to cry. "The phone lines run two ways," I add in Mom's voice, and we laugh together.

"I'll call more often."

"No, you won't." I sniffle. "You're just saying that because you feel bad about treating me like a baby."

I can tell that I've embarrassed him, because his neck turns red and he looks down at his feet.

He says, "You game for a little more shoveling?"

We go outside and before we start shoveling, I toss a handful of snow at him. "Gotcha back."

"So you did, Rosie."

We work in silence. My clothes get so sweaty that they stick to my body. We finish our shoveling, and I follow Marcus to the backyard. He clears snow off the trampoline and then takes off his boots and climbs on. He bounces once, then twice, then high, higher. I listen to his panting and the sound of his wet socks slapping against the canvas. Breath. Splat. Breath. Splat.

I don't want to be left out, so I climb up on the trampoline and plunk down on the cross in the center. Marcus is breathing harder now, and he looks at me like I'm barging in on his fun, like he used to when I tried to talk to his friends as they ran off to a football game and left me home watching *Fantasy Island* with Mom and Dad. I'm not budging, though.

He tries to bounce me, but I'm a lot heavier than I was when I was a kid. Maybe I weigh more than he does now. He jumps, and I just slide around a little.

"Marcus, jump harder!"

He tries again, but I still don't move much.

"Marcus, jump higher!" I scream at him, like our lives depend on whether he can bounce me into the air.

He bounces a few more times, staring at his feet. And then he jumps as high as he possibly can. It's starting to snow again, and I turn my head through the light flakes, toward the kitchen window where Mom's looking on. I look up at Marcus, and for the first time all weekend, maybe the first time since we were kids, he faces me and looks at me hard. I lean my head back and smile at him as he comes down. When he lands, my body moves ever so slightly in the direction of the darkening sky.

LADIES NIGHT

Robin Weiss-Gold, June 2002

Robin wiped a glob of guacamole from the expensive suede jacket she'd bought Marcus for his birthday. Now they couldn't take it back. "I'm sorry," he said for the one hundredth time that week. He was sorry that his bakery's largest account, a hotel chain, had gone bankrupt, and sorry that his retailers had cut their bread orders; thanks to Atkins and South Beach, carbs were the new bubonic plague. He was sorry that he'd tried to save his business by draining their 401Ks and Justin's bar mitzvah savings account.

"No need to be sorry. You can take anything back to Nordstrom," she said brightly, and relayed an anecdote she'd heard about a woman who successfully returned a pair of sandals with a hole in one of the soles. Cheerfulness was Robin's best weapon to fight her mounting anger toward her husband.

"I think I've made too big of a mess." He leaned against the large kitchen island, a brass rack of Calphalon sparkling over his head.

She wet a paper towel and dabbed the stain maniacally. "I think I'm getting it," she said as she constructed the sob story she'd give the saleswoman. Sheila? No, Shelly. She'd tell Shelly that next week the bakery would file for bankruptcy and she and Marcus would lose everything: the house, the trampoline, and the chocolate-colored suede jacket that smelled like success.

He started to reach for her, but he stopped.

"The kids are waiting upstairs for you to help them with their homework," she said. "I'm hosting ladies night, remember?"

Marcus tried to fish a broken Dorito out of the bowl of guacamole. She shooed him away. He'd done enough damage for one night, actually for one lifetime. She poured year-old Halloween candy into a dish. This was the first time ever she hadn't baked for ladies night. And there would be no gourmet pita chips to accompany the unnaturally green artichoke dip from Whole Foods. Too expensive. She opened a bottle of wine and downed a glass. She rarely drank.

Robin gave herself her hourly reminder that she was being a big baby. People went to bed hungry every night all over the world, and here she was whining about having to serve stale candy to a group of well-heeled women? Waa-waa. Her mother would never have spent a week's worth of grocery money on one night of fancy snacks and wine. She lit a thick candle, wishing that the group was gathering around Becca's fire pit tonight. Some time away from the house would do her a world of good. Still, she knew she could count on the ladies to distract her from herself for a few hours, perhaps help her redirect the tropical storm that was brewing along her inner coast.

She put an assortment of *her* music on their CD player: Cowboy Junkies, Indigo Girls, and Tracy Chapman. Woman-power lyrics always perked her up. She barely heard the knock of her sister-in-law, Hannah, orchestrator of this book club that had turned into ladies night because nobody ever read the books.

"I love this song," Hannah said as she entered the kitchen. "Is it Tracy Chapman or Joan Armatrading?"

"Tracy Chapman," Robin said. "Can you really not tell the difference?"

Hannah shrugged, and Robin noticed her new diamond stud earrings. They probably cost more than Robin's mortgage, a thought that never would have occurred to her a few weeks ago. Her brother Danny had always been a generous gift giver, and now he was an enormously successful realtor. After Hannah had Goldie, she'd given up her job running a nonprofit that taught parenting skills to inner-city teens. Too much travel. Robin wouldn't have pegged Hannah as the stay-at-home type, but babies and wealth became her.

"Am I too late to say goodnight to my niece and nephew?" Hannah kissed Robin's cheek. Hannah was still making up for what she called her "uber-bitch" phase, when fertility hormone treatments and pregnancy stress made her too bitter and nervous to bond with Justin and Sydney. Now she was the mother of two girls and hands down the most content person Robin knew. Robin longed for the time when she'd been the happier one.

"Of course not. Maybe *you* can help Justin study for his math test." Robin laughed.

"Oh, I seriously doubt that."

Hannah trotted up the steps while Robin poured herself a second glass of wine. She anticipated that they would either have to rent their house or sell it, move back to Rochester, and live with Marcus's mother for the summer. Esther had already found her a dental hygienist gig. Robin loved her mother-in-law, but the idea of sharing a home with Esther made her breath catch. And what would they tell the kids? Justin had been counting the days until his second summer at a sleepaway camp that had been kind enough to refund their deposit. Sydney had been picking up tension in the house lately and had begun chewing her nails until her fingers bled.

Becca Coopersmith let herself into the house without knocking. "It's just the three of us tonight," she said.

"No Amy?" Robin asked. Hannah's sister worked long hours, but when she did join the group she always entertained them, originally with tales of her romantic escapades and now with wickedly funny commentary on the suburban life she was leading with her new husband, Leon.

"Nope. And Maggie called," Becca said. "Eric had to go up to New York for a shoot." Maggie never left the kids when Eric had a job in Manhattan, not after he'd been on a shoot blocks from Ground Zero when the towers were hit.

Hannah came downstairs. "Justin's math is beyond me, but I did get to see Sydney's new cartwheel. Hey, where's Maggie?"

"Eric's in New York," Becca said.

"Oh." Hannah grabbed a Milky Way from the dish. "Poor baby." She meant Maggie, but Eric was her brother, and she worried about him too.

Robin felt a rush of love for her ladies. She knew they would listen compassionately if she chose to describe the nightmare of the last two weeks, and she knew they would brainstorm about ways to help, but she was too embarrassed by the stigma of going broke and her prior obliviousness to their situations.

Becca and Hannah poured themselves some wine, walked into the great room, and settled into their assigned comfy chairs. Hannah slid off her sandals and wiggled her freshly pedicured feet. Robin kicked off her Danskos and polished off her second glass of wine.

"Okay, so let's get to the important stuff. Did you invite Nikki?" Hannah asked, ready to dine out on Bertrand Court gossip.

"No, I forgot," Robin said, hoping Nikki wouldn't see them through the big living-room window as she launched into a Tad-bashing tirade. A month after the Chamberlains had moved to Bertrand Court, Tad ended up in her dentist's chair, and it took her a full hour to scrape an inordinate amount of plaque from his teeth. He didn't acknowledge her, even though she'd appeared at his front door with a banana bread only the week before. Clearly he didn't have room for a dental hygienist in even the outer periphery of his social circle. Rumor had it that before he and Nikki moved to the neighborhood, they used to ski with the Gores. Now the Republicans were in office, and Tad, out of his White House job, couldn't find work anywhere.

Hannah tucked her feet under her legs. "I saw their new dog. Christ, it's the size of a horse."

"Hugo, I think his name is," Becca said. "He was walking Nikki the other day, and she had to bring a Hefty bag to clean up his poop."

"I can't imagine Nikki cleaning up shit," Hannah said.

"Me neither," Becca agreed. "But I like her."

"Me too, but that doesn't mean we have to stop talking about her," Hannah said.

"Who knows? Maybe she talks about us too?" Becca said.

Robin practically snorted. "Us? I don't think so."

This conversation was not bringing Robin her usual guilty satisfaction. She imagined Tad and Marcus bumping into each other at Starbucks in the middle of the morning, both unemployed and lost. She decided to forgive Tad right then and there for his plaque and arrogance.

Once they got their Tad and Nikki fix out of the way, the women moved on to discussing their summer plans, as it was early June.

"What are you guys up to this summer, Bec?" Hannah asked.

Typically, Becca amused Robin with her unbridled enthusiasm for — well, everything. She'd dragged them all to a steamy yoga studio in the District to sweat their asses off for ninety minutes, but who was counting? She'd lured them into fire-pit bull sessions, belly dancing, Zumba, and the adult bat mitzvah class that Robin had dropped out of. Robin only half listened while Becca described the trip she and Adam were taking to Italy while the boys were off at the same summer camp where Becca and Adam had met.

"Have a gelato for me." Robin's tongue was growing thick

from the wine. She poured herself a third glass.

"Slow down there, girl." Becca put her hand over her own wine glass.

"So tell me, Hannah, where is my fabulous brother taking you and your girls this summer?" Robin tapped her sister-in-law's knee a bit too hard.

Hannah gave Robin a look and twirled her diamond stud around in her ear. "British Columbia."

"And will you be bringing your staff?" Robin tried to sound innocent when she asked the question, but a thorny rim around the word "staff" gave her away.

Hannah looked hurt. "I hadn't planned on it."

Becca glanced from Robin to Hannah and fiddled with the chamsah charm on her necklace. Robin's inner storm was picking up in speed and intensity. The wine was not helping matters. "Excuse me," she said, and got up and went into the kitchen.

She heard Marcus come downstairs and close the door to his office. She was grateful that he didn't stop to say hello to Becca and Hannah. She placed both hands on the counter and drew her shoulders back, the way her physical therapist had taught her, to relieve the muscle spasms that were a casualty of her work. She took a glass out of the cupboard and held it under the Deer Park water dispenser. They'd have to get rid of this forty-dollar-a-month luxury. Robin hadn't worried so much about money since she was a kid and her father went broke after investing in a Ponzi scheme. Danny set out to earn back every penny his dad had lost, and their sister Denise married for money, but Robin decided to learn a trade. People would always need their teeth cleaned. Robin and Marcus had used her meager salary to fund vacations, and she'd also tucked away some money to indulge in expensive gifts for the children, but even if she worked full time, she could never support the family, much less pay off the bakery's debt.

She felt a warm hand on her shoulder. "You okay?" Becca startled her from her thoughts.

Becca stroked her friend's back, the gesture triggering Robin's fierce longing for her mother. She wanted to ask her how they'd managed to survive Daddy's bankruptcy. But both of her parents were dead, and here she was drinking too much wine and sniping at Hannah because of her financial security.

"Let's go back in," she said.

"Okay, then," Becca said, and they returned to the great room.

Robin removed a Hershey's Kiss from the dish and handed it to Hannah. "Peace offering," she mumbled. There, she could be nice. Maybe the storm was going to die down and not hit land at all.

"It's okay," Hannah said, but Robin could tell she was still hurt.

"God, I'm sorry I've been such a bitch. Forgive the PMS, ladies."

Hannah gave the Kiss back to Robin. "Maybe you need the chocolate more than I do."

"You're right, Han." Robin stroked her sister-in-law's arm.

Becca and Hannah wore sympathy all over their faces. Robin was tempted to confide in them with the childish hope that Hannah would suggest wanding Danny's money at the problem and everything would return to normal. Then she remembered a book club discussion — back when they read the books — about a woman who had denied her mentally ill brother financial assistance. Hannah had been the lone member to side with main character. "My dad told me never to lend large sums of money to relatives. It caused all sorts of weirdness between my grandmother and Aunt Sylvia," she'd said, and Robin had filed away the comment. Now her face grew hot, and little beads of sweat pooled on her cheeks. She smiled as warmly as she could at Hannah, again taking in her earrings, as well as the Tumi bag nestled beside her.

"I think I'll feel better with a good night's sleep," Robin chirped.

"I bet you will," Hannah said, but Robin could tell she'd thrown Hannah off her game. They all put their shoes back on and took their wine glasses into the kitchen. Becca put her hand on the chair where Marcus had flung his jacket. "Oh, is this the one you bought him for his birthday?" She picked up the jacket and ogled it, trying to break the tension in the room. Her eyes moved in the direction of the guacamole stain, but she didn't say anything.

"Nice addition, huh?" Robin said.

"Let me give you the name of a fantastic dry cleaner," Becca offered.

"I think it's hopeless." Robin wanted to cry, but she laughed instead. She hated this new laugh. It was obnoxious.

Hannah and Becca looked at her more lovingly than ever.

"Come on, I'll walk you out," Robin said.

Robin walked the two of them past the trampoline and

the green Adirondack chairs. When they reached the end of the driveway, she said, "Good night, ladies," and released them into the darkness.

"Poor baby," Hannah muttered as she walked Becca to her front door.

Robin awoke the next morning with a pounding headache and wine breath. She crawled under the covers to block out Marcus instructing the kids to let Mommy sleep instead of kissing her goodbye when they left for school. She got out of bed at ten o'clock, brushed her teeth, gargled with Listerine, showered, and went downstairs. She knocked on the open door of Marcus's office and stepped in. He was sitting at his desk, staring at his computer. He looked drawn. Up until a year ago, he'd maintained his wrestler's physique. Now he just looked like a skinny little man. Robin glanced over his shoulder and saw the bankruptcy attorney's name on an email message.

"How do you feel this morning?" Marcus asked, not looking up from the screen.

"Too much wine."

She walked over to his filing cabinet and opened the drawer that held their credit card receipts. Robin barely used her personal credit card, so it wasn't hard to locate the receipt for Marcus's jacket. The fatter envelope traced all her purchases for the family: the new set of pots and pans from Williams-Sonoma, expensive yoga pants from Lucy for herself, gymnastics classes for Sydney, and tuition to basketball camp for Justin. How could she have been so blind to what was going on with Marcus? Why hadn't he confided in her? Marcus didn't know how to ask for help. She should have pushed harder when he started to wear his worry on his face. When she'd tried to comfort him initially, he'd just said that he was sad about losing his father. She'd known there was more to it all along.

She felt him standing behind her, and she whispered, "Please don't say you're sorry again."

"I won't." He sounded defensive, as if she'd called him a bad name.

"I'm going to run an errand, okay?" She turned around to face him, but they both avoided eye contact.

She went to the hall closet and retrieved a Nordstrom shopping bag. When she entered the kitchen, she discovered that the jacket was not hanging over the chair. "Marcus?" she hollered.

"What's wrong?" he said, rushing into the kitchen.

"Where's the jacket?"

"I put it in the dry-cleaning basket. I think you did the best you could with the stain, babe. I'll take it in later."

"Don't do that. Then we're stuck with it for good," she said too sharply, and kissed his cheek to make up for her impatience. He needed her support right now, she had to remember that.

"Okay, Robin."

"I'll be back soon," she said, and waited for Marcus to slink back to his office. Then she rescued the jacket from the dry cleaning, put it in the Nordstrom bag with the receipt, and slipped out the back door, her wet hair dampening the collar of her shirt.

The car practically drove itself to the mall. Her stomach growled fiercely as she walked into Nordstrom, past the lingerie mannequins and up the escalator to the men's department. A young man in a black suit played "Just the Way You Are" on the grand piano adjacent to the kids' department, and the song mixed with the din of the store, jangling her last nerve.

She recognized the saleswoman as soon as she stepped into the coat section. "Hi, Shelly," she said.

"I remember you!" said Shelly with a big smile that revealed her professionally whitened teeth. She seemed flattered that Robin recalled her name. "Tell me, tell me, how did your hubby like the jacket?" she asked, as if they were in cahoots.

Robin's eyes filled with tears, and she took a deep breath. "I actually have some sad news."

"Come here." Shelly guided Robin away from a salesman talking loudly with a customer.

Robin followed her, and when they reached the cash register, she let Shelly take her hand. "My husband won't be wearing this coat," she said, sniffling.

Shelly squeezed Robin's fingers.

"Our family has suffered a devastating loss."

Shelly's own eyes teared up, and Robin could see the layers of eye shadow she'd expertly applied to her upper lid. Robin had never gotten the hang of eye shadow.

"Oh, God. I'm so sorry," Shelly said.

"This is too painful of a reminder." Robin held out the bag.

Shelly took it, stuck her hand inside, and retrieved the receipt. "Give me your card, sweetie."

Robin handed over her credit card slowly, hoping that Shelly wouldn't remove the stained garment from the bag.

Shelly fished her reading glasses from her breast pocket and began pecking away at her computer. "Do you want me to put this back on your card?" she asked softly.

For a second, Robin doubted herself. She didn't want Shelly to have to absorb the cost of the ruined jacket. Shelly didn't deserve to suffer for Marcus's mistakes. That was wrong. But then again, Nordstrom's return policy was so generous that they likely threw away hundreds of items they couldn't resell. She bit her lip. "No, I think I'll take the cash, if that's okay."

"Of course," Shelly said, and she pulled $342.63 from the register.

"Thank you," Robin murmured, taking the cash. The weight of the wad of bills made her feel safe.

Shelly came around from behind the counter and hugged Robin hard.

Robin returned the hug gratefully, surprised that she could gobble up affection from someone to whom she'd so blatantly lied. She liked Shelly's perfume, a mix of citrus and jasmine.

When Shelly eventually released her, Robin thanked her again and went back down the elevator. She loosened her fist around the cash and pulled her wallet out of her purse,

thinking that this money would buy a week's worth of groceries and a new gymnastics leotard for Sydney. Then she
dropped the wallet back into the bottom of her bag, slid the
cash into the front pocket of her jeans, and walked out of the
store with her hand clutched to her thigh.

WOULD YOU RATHER?

Nikki Chamberlain, November 2002

Lately Nikki finds herself one weather system behind. Yesterday it was cold, and Emma's teacher admonished her for sending the child to school in shorts. Today it's balmy, and Nikki smells like sweaty wool. To cool down, she holds a glass of ice water against her cheek while she watches for Georgia. The past few times they've met for their monthly dinners, the sitter didn't show or Tad forgot to come home early, and Nikki arrived frazzled and apologizing profusely to Georgia, whose general unflappability only made her prattle on more.

Raindrops the size of cashews pelt the window, snaking down tall sheets of glass painted with faded red letters that read "Rodeo's," the hot spot of their youth. Too early for the mariachi band. She rifles through a wooden bowl for an unbroken chip, relishing the taste of oil and salt on her tongue. Tad, the fat-gram zealot, stopped eating chips when he became addicted to triathlon training. She needs to call him before the girls go to bed.

"Hi, Nik." She loves Tad's voice; it exudes both authority and playfulness, almost a twinkle, as if he could run a perfect press conference one minute and crack you up with a well-told joke the next. As he has.

She detects the sound of *Lizzie McGuire* playing in the background, annoyed that Tad's chosen to plunk Sophie and Emma in front of the television instead of engaging them with a puzzle or a game. He's probably reading *Triathlete* magazine or doing push-ups or his back exercises. She selects her words carefully. "Hi, honey, just wanted to let you know where I put Sophie's antibiotic." She tries to sound helpful instead of nagging.

"Kitchen windowsill," he replies, slightly winded, probably from the push-ups.

Well, at least he noticed the bottle. "Good day?" She uses the noncommittal tone she's practiced with the girls when she wants them to give her more than a grunt. She doesn't ask if he sent out any résumés or made any follow-up calls. Doesn't offer up any leads she's shaken down from her old colleagues on the Democratic Leadership Council.

"Fine." His voice is tight.

She can picture the defensiveness creeping into his eyes, as it does whenever she tries to help him resuscitate his career. "Kiss the girls. Goodnight, sweetie." She hangs up before he can answer.

Tad. She fiddles with her wedding band. He lost his in the gym locker room last spring and never bothered replacing it. And two weeks ago, when they dined at a pan-Asian restaurant with a big dairy lobbyist, a friend of a friend of Nikki's who ended up not hiring the "way overqualified" Tad, he revised the lore of how they met. He said he almost missed meeting

Nikki because he was groping around the beer-soaked floor of a Capitol Hill bar with a pretty brunette, helping her find a contact lens. Minor, really, but he'd never used the verb "groping" or the adjective "pretty" before. These details gnaw at her more than the missing wedding band.

With the help of a little sangria, she ushers the emerging Tad unpleasantness into the recesses of her consciousness, periodically glancing at the hostess stand in search of Georgia. The restaurant is practically empty, except for a young woman — roughly Nikki's age when she and Georgia lived up the street and referred to Rodeo's as "the Cafeteria" — sitting two booths over, encouraging a middle-aged man to ply her with margaritas. The girl, serviceably pretty, wears pointy shoes and a gray wraparound dress that might have looked nice on Nikki once. Every few seconds, her hand darts to her hair — blue-black like Nikki's — and brushes it from her eyes. This isn't one of those ego-stroking career-advancement dinners Nikki used to endure when she could still leverage her cleavage and tight skin. No, this girl is intrigued. She laughs too loudly at his jokes; her cheeks redden when he touches her wrist, which he does often, with the ringless fingers of his right hand. Nikki knows her laugh and his touch.

———

Fifteen years ago, on a cold March night, shortly after Nikki and Georgia had settled into their first post-college apartment, Nikki waited for Georgia at an Irish bar one block down from Rodeo's, at 17th and S. Now it's a tapas restaurant. She'd been working for the Murphy Group advertising agency for two months when her boss informed her of their St. Patrick's Day tradition: employees were expected to make an appearance at the Irish Times to drink green beer and act inappropriately with colleagues.

The men wore kelly-green ties decorated with four-leaf clovers or leprechauns. Nikki wore her new black pumps, which were torturing her feet, and an Ann Taylor suit, a micromini, a fashion must in the late eighties. Lucky for Nikki that she had nice legs.

She tried not to glaze over as she listened to an account executive describe in detail how he was house-training his new black lab; she asked perfunctory follow-up questions, all the while keeping one eye open for Georgia. She'd just had another fight with Nate, her college boyfriend, who was moving to Moldova in June. Peace Corps. He mimicked her feminist diatribes (she was an insufferably enthusiastic women's studies major) while he watched her slide into her short skirts and pumps each morning. Thinking about Nate made her angry and sad and nostalgic for the time when they both believed that Nikki wanted to spend three years in some underdeveloped country doing good. She needed a drink.

"I'll have a Maker's Mark, please. And a 7UP." She smiled at the bartender, who winked at her and turned away to fix her drink. She downed the whole thing in four gulps.

"That's a mean cocktail for a lovely young lady like yourself." Jack O'Dell, senior vice-president of the Murphy Group, gave her that pre–Monica Lewinsky head-to-toe once-over. She'd noticed him before; he was Frame Guy, a hot, fiftyish, mildly weathered sort dressed in a fishing sweater and faded jeans, a dead ringer for the model in the picture frame she bought last Christmas. She had pet names for lots of the people who worked for the Murphy Group: I'm Not Your Mother cleaned out the office fridge every Friday, bitching and moaning the whole time; Q-Tip cleaned his ear with a paper clip and then scraped the wax onto his desk calendar; and Boner Man — well, no explanation necessary.

She tilted her head slightly to one side and looked directly into his eyes, a play she'd stolen from the January issue of *Cosmopolitan*. He had big, square white teeth and a dimple in his chin, slightly darkened by some recalcitrant stubble.

"What's your name, kid?"

"You have a kind face," she said. That was the Maker's Mark talking, not *Cosmo*. Idiot. Why did she say that? Even if it seemed true?

"Have I now?" he said with a smile.

"Nikki, I'm Nikki O'Neill. No relation to Tip," she added lamely.

"Let's get you another drink, Nikki O'Neill, no relation to Tip."

It wasn't hard to get him talking about himself, but then Nikki had always known how to listen to men, make them feel understood, heard. And contrary to Nate's accusations, she didn't do it just to suck up; she was really interested.

Two drinks later, Jack was telling her a story about his first client, a grumpy old tire dealer out in Falls Church. "He had piles and piles of ad money from Goodyear, just sitting there waiting for someone to help him spend it." His eyes lit up.

"That's the Reliable Tires account?" Nikki knew every

account in the agency, inside and out.

"You do your homework." He nodded with approval, touching her sleeve. "I'll be back in a minute."

Nikki watched him walk toward the men's room. He moved like an ex-football player, stiff in the shoulders, lumbering, but with a healthy dose of confidence in what his body could still do. She had forgotten all about Georgia (and her toes, which ached like she'd just visited a foot binder), until she felt a tug on her sleeve.

"Sorry I'm late. Got stuck editing for the neurotic producer." Georgia removed her glasses and wiped away the condensation that had formed from the heat of the bar.

"Here." Nikki pointed to an empty bar stool next to hers. Georgia had once told her that she hated standing in crowded places because she was so short that she always felt like she had her nose in other people's armpits. She detested going out in general, preferring to sit at home and read a Jane Austen novel. Nikki liked to do both; she'd had a premonition that she would meet her mate at a party. She loved Nate, but he was no Mr. Darcy.

Jack returned from the bathroom, running his hand through his thick head of gray hair. Nikki hoped that Georgia wouldn't notice his wedding band, but of course she would.

"This is my roommate, Georgia. We met in college. Same dorm." Okay, Nikki, slow it down. Stop talking so much. Less is more. "Colgate. Colgate University. In Hamilton. New York. Upstate." Shut up, for Christ's sake.

Georgia gave Nikki one of her Georgia looks, as if she could see right into her brain. Nikki shrugged. God, she was just flirting, having some fun. Sometimes she wished Georgia would flirt a little more, maybe even care about the guys she brought home, like the news photographer with shoulder-length hair who sat at their kitchen table now and then, slurping milk from a cereal bowl. It was almost as if she was completely happy sitting on the sidelines, watching Nikki get drunk and stupid, watching crime victims cry and politicians woo in the news stories she edited.

"Well, Nikki, I'll leave you in Georgia's hands, then. Welcome to the Murphy Group." Before he turned toward the door, he snuck a peek at her legs, which she had twisted around each other like a couple of Twizzlers.

Georgia followed his glance, watched him leave, and gave her friend another look.

"What?" Nikki shifted on her stool.

"Would you rather have a Pap smear or a root canal?"

Nikki laughed. Would You Rather was a game they'd started playing their freshman year of college, a tacit agreement to distract themselves from the subject of, say, Nikki's mother's cancer or Georgia's top-secret affair with her philosophy professor.

"With or without Novocain?" she said.

"With."

Nikki downed the remains of her drink and paused for effect. "The Pap, no question."

The next day, Georgia was working the late-night shift at her television station and wouldn't be home until after two a.m., which left Nikki free to get into some mischief. She'd picked a silly fight with Nate that morning, sparking a chain of events: Nate took the early bus to Manhattan for his Peace Corps orientation instead of staying to resolve the argument; Nikki chose to work late over catching a step aerobics class at the Y; and when Jack O'Dell pulled out of the parking garage, she was standing at its mouth, shivering in her flimsy suede jacket, and gladly accepted his offer to drive her home.

"You must be freezing." Jack cranked up the heat in his car and moved his gym bag from Nikki's floor mat, brushing her knee with his fingers.

"Thanks. The temperature must have dropped a hundred degrees since this morning." The car smelled like Dentyne and Polo Sport.

"Your teeth are chattering, Nikki O'Neill, no relation to Tip."

"Maybe." Nikki smiled through her quivering lips, thinking about how much Nate would hate Jack. He'd call him corporate scum.

During the three and a half miles between the Murphy Group and Capitol Hill, they talked about Marion Barry's failure to fix potholes and whether he could beat his drug habit. Nikki wanted to keep driving and listen to Jack talk and laugh. He had a great laugh, spontaneous and with lots of bass.

He adjusted his collar — crisp, white, and expensive, in contrast to the yellowed short-sleeved shirt Nate wore with his one tie when he took her out for lunch last week. She hated herself for hurrying both of them out of the building so she wouldn't have to introduce him around.

"You hungry?" Jack looked at her out of the corner of his eye.

Nikki felt her cheeks tingle. Had he just asked her to dinner? "Yeah, a little."

"Take me to your favorite restaurant." He smiled. "It's the least I can do for working you so hard."

"Okay, turn left here." She directed him to a Cuban place she loved, a dive that would be empty at this hour. She glanced at his wedding ring, knowing he would appreciate her discretion, and surprised at how intuitively the etiquette for dining with a married man came to her.

"Got any Scotch?" he asked the pretty waitress, who spoke very little English.

Scotch? Ick. Nikki suddenly wanted to be home cuddled up with Nate under her down comforter, waiting for the water to boil for their Top Ramen, or better yet, sitting at the kitchen table in her sweats, keeping Georgia company while she tested a new recipe from the *Post*.

Jack looked at the waitress, who seemed confused, and then at Nikki. "Right, right. This is a Mexican restaurant. Give me a margarita, por favor."

Beam me up, Scotty. "I'll have a mojito," she said, a bit too politely. When the waitress left, she whispered, "This is a Cuban restaurant."

He laughed with his whole body, shrugging his shoulders and throwing his head back. "God, I'm a dope sometimes. Did I embarrass you?"

"Totally." She loved that he didn't care that the joke was on him. No wonder he was so masterful at charming clients. How could she not like him?

Nikki took charge of the ordering, and the food arrived swiftly.

"Oh, my God." He closed his eyes and sucked on a plantain. "This is damn good. Are these fried bananas?"

"Plantains." She dipped one in the sour cream and fed him.

He took a sip of his second margarita. "So, a looker like you must have a boyfriend."

A looker? Nikki's *dad* used that term. "Let's just have fun tonight," she said. How Helen Gurley Brown of her to take control of the evening, to brush their respective romantic entanglements to the side.

He persisted. "Still got your college boyfriend?"

Nikki recoiled, as if he had asked, "Still sleep with your retainer?" She glanced around for the waitress and crossed her legs, kicking him lightly by accident.

He smiled. "Mysterious, aren't you?"

"Yes, I'm very mysterious." She winked. Where was this coming from?

They didn't talk about the office gossip she'd been collecting at happy hours, like the pending merger or Jack's partners' campaign to force him out. Instead, Jack told her about his first job, selling radio time for a big, fat, ornery manager of a country-western station, and described what it was like to don an orange vest, sip whiskey, and wait for the leaves to rustle with the promise of an eight-pointer. His eyes softened, his fingers tracing the rim of his glass, his back shaking off the tension of the day, of the life. A man clearly used to directing a conversation, he stopped every few minutes, as if he'd been woken from a nap, and asked, "Do you really want to hear all this?" Nikki nodded, taking him in. He seemed lonely, like he needed something from her.

"I haven't done this in years." He looked shy.

Oh, you and your wife don't date other people? she almost said, but discretion trumped sass and rum, so she only smiled and watched him sign for the check.

When they got to his car, she stood next to him, arm to arm, a full head shorter than he was. The wind cut through her jacket, but she was too drunk to care. She felt around in her purse for the bag of Cadbury Easter Eggs she'd bought at the lobby store that day during her lunch break and held one out to him.

"No thanks." He looked at her as though everything she did was amusing.

She felt amusing. "Right. You're driving."

He opened the car door for her, and she arranged herself in the padded leather passenger seat, ignoring her skirt sliding up her thighs. She peeled the foil off the egg and began to eat it one layer at a time: first the pastel-colored candy coating, and then the thick layer of chocolate beneath, and finally the core of a crunchy malted milk ball the size of a marble.

He grinned at her. "I've never seen anyone eat a piece of chocolate like that."

"Try it."

"Okay. Give me one." He stretched out his hand, unwrapped the egg, and licked the purple candy coating, his brow furrowed in concentration.

She giggled.

"What's funny?" He raised one eyebrow.

"Your lavender lips."

He licked the sugar off his lips, laughing, and started the car, jutting out his chin in time with a Creedence song that came blasting from the radio. He looked free, boyish, and comfortable in Nikki's presence.

"Here." She pointed to her apartment building, and he pulled into a coveted spot a block down from her entrance, right in front of a broken streetlight. Kismet. He put the car in park.

"You're a great girl, Nikki."

High on mojitos and her hold on this man, she ran her fingers along the side of his face. A face unlike those of the boys she'd been with up until this point. The skin felt craggy beneath her hand. He looked old and vulnerable and very much hers for the taking. She leaned over and kissed him, tasting the chocolate. They alternately deflowered the Cadbury eggs and kissed until Nikki's stash ran out, giggling like children home from a night of trick-or-treating, sneaking extra candy, dancing on the sofa, daring their parents to stop them.

It wasn't until they were on the last egg that Nikki noticed the keychain that had been dangling in front of her the whole time, a photograph of his family tucked safely inside a rectangular plastic case. Clad in matching Hawaiian shirts, Jack and his teenage son sandwiched a willowy redhead with a purple lily in her hair.

The mojitos and plantains threatened to make an encore. Bad karma she was creating here. She'd pay for this one day. In blood. "Better go." She kissed him on the cheek.

"Let me walk you to your door." His voice turned businesslike, almost fatherly, as though he could erase whatever had happened between them if he wished.

"You watch too much local news," she said over her shoulder as she hoisted herself out of his car and ran to her apartment, trying not to think of the liquor store two blocks down that had been robbed last week, or of Jack's wife waiting for him in their cold bed, or of Nate listening to bad folk music in some bar in the Village, or that she was minutes from throwing up an evening of excess.

She was still camped out on the pink furry rug in the bathroom when Georgia came home from work. "I'm ill," she groaned. "Very, very ill."

Georgia refrained from commenting that the bathroom smelled like a still. "Did you take aspirin?"

Nikki knew Georgia wouldn't ply her with questions. Georgia kept quiet when she sensed Nikki had a story to tell. She said nothing as she reached into the medicine cabinet for the aspirin bottle.

"Would you rather date a married man or ingest a tub of Crisco?" Nikki asked, still a little drunk.

"Choose the Crisco, Nikki." Georgia dampened a washcloth with cold water and held it to Nikki's neck.

During the half hour leading up to Nikki's final siege of vomiting, she swore that she'd become the kind of person who would glance at that photo of Jack's lovely wife and never speak to him again. She would call Nate and tell him that she'd go wherever the Peace Corps chose to send him and end her love affair with Washington and all its charms. The moment passed, and for the balance of Jack's wife's conference in Hilton Head, Nate's training in the Big Apple, and Georgia's turn working the late shift — three days total — Nikki and Jack ate and drank at passé watering holes and traded kisses in his car while his key chain dangled inches shy of his groin.

————

Georgia finally arrives at Rodeo's, soaking wet, glasses foggy, brown turtleneck accentuating her breasts, elasticity intact. She's aged well, better than Nikki. She apologizes for her tardiness without explanation, but Nikki guesses that she lost track of time in her windowless editing suite. Georgia would never brag — she hates talking about herself — but Nikki learned from a neighbor that Georgia's a big deal in the documentary world, that one of her films was nominated for an Emmy last spring. These films are Georgia's children, Nikki persuades herself when she's staving off the occasional pang of jealousy.

Georgia kisses Nikki on the cheek and orders a glass of wine. The mariachi band has arrived; Nikki's sweater has dried and she's energized by her foray into her past. She fancies herself Nikki O'Neill, no relation to Tip, star Democratic rainmaker, charmer of powerful men like Jack O'Dell. She's animated when she serves up amusing yet self-deprecating tales of her attempts to train Hugo, whom she hates.

"You loathe dogs," Georgia says.

"Gives Tad's life some purpose." Nikki pours herself another glass of sangria and looks away. "I didn't just say that."

Georgia never offers false comfort like "He'll find

something" or "It will all work out" or "Let me ask Jim or Marcus or Skip if they can make a few phone calls." She looks at Nikki with that expressionless, nonjudgmental Georgia look that's always given Nikki's other friends the willies. Nikki regains her composure, and they discuss Georgia's new film on recidivism.

After the waiter places a fresh bowl of salsa on the table, Nikki offers up a few of the girls' funny little observations on life. An Austen purist, she rants about a film adaptation of *Sense and Sensibility* she rented last weekend. A dazzling résumé, a dog-loving husband, smart kids, superior taste in literature — she's hoping that the young woman wearing the gray wraparound dress is eavesdropping on her conversation and has recognized that Nikki has it all.

"You're in a mood tonight." Georgia stares at Nikki.

In an attempt to recapture her good spirits, Nikki points her chin in the direction of the girl, who is now cocking her head, listening intently to the older man regaling her with a tale, probably one that features himself as the hero. "Who do they remind you of?" Nikki starts to grin, sure that Georgia will call up her man-eating days and Jack O'Dell.

Georgia pauses and stares at the couple thoughtfully while Nikki fights the urge to give hints. "The woman could be any ambitious Capitol Hill nubile."

Nikki swallows her grin, reeling from Georgia's unintentional sucker punch.

Still focused on the couple, Georgia narrows her eyes, examining the handsome man. "And him? That's a no-brainer."

Nikki's neck reddens. She wonders if Georgia even

remembers Jack O'Dell.

"He's Tad." Georgia reaches for a chip.

Nikki swivels her head toward the man. Yes, she can see the resemblance: same business casual slacks, same fading tan, same "I'm in charge" wink to the waitress, same empty eyes. Eyes that crave the adulation Tad now receives from his training buddies, who join him in squandering their family time with long runs, long naps, long bike rides. Eyes that crave the sexual hunger that drained from her body with her breast milk and the energy it's taken to prop him up. But this man wears a wedding ring, and Tad no longer does, which now bothers her.

Georgia glances at Nikki's doppelgänger with a look of recognition and a poor attempt to mask her pity.

Nikki steals a sip of Georgia's water and swallows, rinsing her mouth of the taste of sangria, once sweet, now all alcohol and bitterness from the orange rind. She tries too hard to sound flip when she says, "Would you rather be blind or invisible?"

The mariachi band begins to play to the near-empty restaurant, too festive and off key, but loud enough to drown out Georgia's answer and the rain and the laughter of the couple two tables over.

HARVARD MAN

Tad Chamberlain, July 2003

My wife, Nikki, and I have our most enthusiastic sex on the nights when Georgia comes over for dinner, which hasn't been for a long time. She's due here in twenty minutes, and I'm still sweating like a swine from biking down to the Jefferson Memorial, twenty-three miles roundtrip.

I peel off my jersey and contemplate the unopened package of razor blades sitting next to the bathroom sink. Who will notice if I don't shave? Georgia Dumfries. Nikki and I have never discussed it, but we habitually pose for her friend's cameralike gaze. Nikki will kiss me hello tenderly on the lips, or I'll pick up one of my daughters and swing her over my head until she belly laughs. Small embellishments like that. And after Georgia leaves, we'll stretch out on our king-size bed and agree that she deserves to find a good man, because beneath her reserve she's warm and kind. We'll run through the tired, diminishing list of our single friends and come up with nobody for her. And then we'll sigh, and Nikki's breathing will quicken, and we'll ravage each other like we did during our early courtship, when we spent full Sundays in the bedroom of the apartment she shared with Georgia, who likely heard our every groan and giggle through the paper-thin walls. Things shift around in my biking shorts in anticipation of the end of the evening.

I run a hot shower to loosen up my quad muscles. Too many hills today. I'm getting old, a thought I brush aside, along with the phone call I received from my college roommate yesterday, telling me that he's running for the Senate. He'll win too. Goddamned chads. I'm on my third job since Dubya stole Florida. Lobbyists used to dribble my name like a basketball; the Gores showed up at the kids' christening (they gave us two BabyBjörns, which we still keep, even though the girls just turned seven).

I raise the water temperature, and the combination of the scalding heat and my endorphin buzz anesthetizes me, for now anyway. Through a thickening mist, I see Nikki come in and open the medicine cabinet. I haven't seen that blouse since early in our marriage, when I got jealous as hell the night she wore it to a dinner meeting with a charming Midwestern real estate mogul. She didn't need to rely on a tight blouse to make gallons of rain for the Democrats. The first Thanksgiving we spent in Phoenix, she almost persuaded her uncle Richard — Barry Goldwater's drinking buddy, no less — to write a check to the Clinton campaign.

When the water turns tepid, I open the shower door and Nikki faces me through the scrim of steam. Nursing two babies stole the perkiness from her breasts, and her blouse pulls between the middle buttons, revealing a dingy beige bra. "Here," she says, offering me a Gatorade with her jaunty smile, which during the early days of my professional purgatory meant something besides pity and resignation.

"Georgia!" She's always prompt. I mean to kiss her cheek, but she moves her head and my lips land on a patch of her wiry hair. She's contributed her usual brick of Stilton cheese toward dessert. She and Nikki remind me of the women I knew in college who read a lot of George Eliot and Margaret Drabble and drank tea instead of Diet Coke in the late afternoon.

The kitchen smells like mint and garlic and Nikki's lilacs, which puts me in a festive mood. Nikki opens the back door and in bounds Hugo, our German shepherd–lab mix. He pounces on Georgia, who's built like a slightly bottom-heavy Eastern European gymnast, and knocks her off balance. A true cat person, Georgia recoils.

"Down, Hugo," Nikki orders without conviction. It's been months since Hugo joined the family, and she still hasn't learned how to control him. She feebly grabs his collar, and he tugs her shoulder toward him. She looks up at her friend. "That green suits you. You should wear pastels more often. The girls used to love it when I wore pink, the official princess color. Who would have thought? Runs against the grain of my inner feminist," Nikki prattles on to Georgia, which is easy to do, since Georgia always waits a few seconds after you finish talking before she responds.

"Girls, Georgia's here," Nikki calls.

Georgia and I follow her to the family room, where the twins, scrubbed and dressed in matching pajamas, are parallel reading *Harry Potter and the Chamber of Secrets.*

"Hi, Sophie," Georgia says. "Which do you like better, Slytherin or Gryffindor?" She gets her name right on the first try, when even my mother can't tell the girls apart if they're wearing the same thing.

"Gryffindor," Sophie answers shyly.

"Slytherin's mean," Emma pipes up.

I tug lightly at their ponytails. "In this house, you've got to keep up with your Hogwarts trivia," I tease. Then I kiss my daughters goodnight, and they head upstairs with Nikki.

Georgia examines me. She hasn't seen me since I started working out, and damn it feels good to be back to my fighting weight: 174 pounds.

"I hear you're competing in triathlons." She dips a carrot stick into Nikki's famous and labor-intensive artichoke dip. "Sounds like a lot of work."

"Not if you love it. I swim with a masters team at the crack of dawn, over at Hains Point. I can usually squeeze a four- or five-mile hoof on the Mall into my lunch hour, and weekends are for long rides." When I describe my routine to Georgia, it sounds more self-indulgent than impressive. "I signed up for a half Ironman in Texas in late fall," I add for no reason.

Thank God Nikki appears. She gives a little clap. "Let me show off my peonies before it gets dark." We follow her into the garden, where the cicadas are screeching in cadence. I love summer.

Georgia bends over to sniff a pink flower, nodding in appreciation. "Remember that orchid you stole from Perry Eisenfeld's wedding?"

She means Perry Eisenstadt; he had a thing for Nikki when he worked for her. She wore stilettos to his wedding, which gave her a good inch on me. Sexy. After a few gin and tonics, she led the guests in a plucky if less than graceful version of the electric slide. A couple of hours later, I held her hair while she retched from an unfortunate encounter with a shrimp cocktail. Luckily for me, I'm allergic to shellfish. Luckily for me, she decided to marry me that night.

Nikki smiles wistfully, fingering the pendant I gave her for our tenth anniversary. "Seems like another lifetime."

We return to the den to find that Hugo has polished off the artichoke dip. Nikki and I exchange glances. Mine says, "He never would have gobbled up *my* artichoke dip." Nikki's says, "I'm working on it, Tad." And even though we haven't spoken, I feel like Georgia has heard every word of our conversation.

I clear the spotless — thanks to Hugo — dip bowl, a wedding gift that we rarely use anymore. These days, we mainly invite other families over for pizza. The energy is different when it's just Georgia, who almost always arrives solo. After the twins were born, she showed up with a manic bass player who looked like an exterminator but apparently oozed sex appeal onstage. He lost his charm when he tried to light up in our living room, only a few feet from our dozing infants. Georgia's visits grew less frequent after that.

Nikki is sprinkling dried cranberries on the salad when Georgia asks me about my new job.

"I write a lot of op-eds, even though people are about as excited to read about health-care issues as they are to hear the details of someone's Disney vacation, in real time." I chuckle, more out of truth than self-deprecation.

Nikki gives me a courtesy laugh. She used to love my analogies.

"I'm the number-two guy at the association, so I have quite a bit of freedom." Code word for boredom, but the money is good, and I haven't had to give up much training time.

Nikki adds brightly, "One of Tad's Harvard buddies wants him to coauthor a book."

Ever since my career went on life support, Nikki's been sneaking my Harvard degree into conversations: "When Tad lived in Cambridge..." or "He graduated with Tad, Harvard, class of '82..." or "Tommy Lee Jones lived in Tad's dorm...." She used to drop the H-bomb to mock her snotty little pedigree-happy DLC staffers, back when we were a power couple. Now she says these things without irony.

Hugo interrupts us by barking at some neighbors strolling past our dining room window. "Hugo," I command. He quiets down immediately, and I rub his belly with my foot.

Georgia nods toward the dog. "So are the girls helping with him?"

Nikki's pale blue eyes reveal amusement. "Hugo is definitely Tad's puppy. They run together in Rock Creek Park, and then he takes him to Starbucks." In a singsongy voice, she crafts an entire album of Kodak moments for her friend, as if she's composing our annual Christmas letter.

"Hugo would be your dog too, love, if you asserted yourself." I sound like I'm scolding one of our daughters.

Nikki sighs dramatically. "Are we going to have this alpha-rolling squabble again?" Another Georgia thing we do is stage fake arguments for her to settle. "Tell me what you think of this, Georgia. Tad's upset with me because I refuse to alpha-roll the dog."

"Alpha-roll?" Georgia raises an eyebrow over her glasses.

My enthusiasm for this topic crackles like a hot tin of Jiffy Pop. I describe how I stumbled upon a book called *How to Be Your Dog's Best Friend*, written by the monks of New Skete. They based their advice on scientific studies of wolf behavior conducted in the 1940s.

"Georgia, you may know from editing nature documentaries that dogs order themselves, like wolves." I take a sip of wine, which goes straight to my head after my long bike ride. "You've got to show the dog that you're dominant, or alpha. That's the only way they'll listen to you." My voice is loud.

Georgia adjusts her glasses and blinks. "So have you alpha-rolled Hugo?"

"I have." I look at my wife. "Nik won't do it." This is Georgia's cue to offer an obvious solution to our discord, granting the illusion that we've acquiesced to her idea and not to each other.

Instead she furrows her brow. "What does it entail?"

Despite her soft voice, I feel like she's putting me on the witness stand, and I don't like being challenged. "You flip the dog onto his back and hold him in that submissive position, sometimes by the throat, and then you growl at his jugular."

"This works?"

"Have you noticed how Hugo only responds to my commands?"

Georgia pauses for her usual few seconds, during which I assume she's registering my wise choice of technique. "Doesn't this traumatize the dog?"

Did she hear me say that a group of fucking monks thought this up?

Nikki scoops up a stray walnut with her fingers. "That's right, Georgia. I knew you'd go to bat for me."

"Make that you and Hugo." Georgia puts her salad fork on her plate with finality.

People don't listen to me like they used to. I even caught an intern, a little sorority girl from the University of Alabama, playing Sudoku while I led a staff meeting. This just didn't happen when I worked four offices down from the President. The anger I numb daily with exercise is pitching a tent in my gullet like a Bedouin in a sandstorm.

Georgia helps Nikki clear the salad plates while I hunt through the refrigerator for another bottle of wine. Nikki reaches out to stroke my arm, but I move away from her. The last thing I need right now is her propping.

"Here, Georgia." She hands her friend a bag of feta to sprinkle on the eggplant dish and then removes a pan of Greek chicken from the oven. "Did I tell you that Becca Coopersmith is taking a pole-dancing class?" She's trying to maneuver the conversation to safer terrain. Nikki has been feeding stories about Becca to Georgia for a while.

"Striptease pole dancing or folk pole dancing?" Georgia's tone is sardonic.

"The former." Nikki giggles.

"Is she still having the adult bat mitzvah?"

"Yeah. Ooh, this is hot." Nikki puts the Pyrex pan on the stove. "All in the name of self-actualization. Becca takes *very* good care of herself."

I love the bite in her voice; I miss the random moments of bitchiness she used to reserve for me alone. "Well, all that dancing melts that middle-aged sag, like a slab of butter on a hotcake," I say, glancing toward Nikki's belly, focusing my gaze on the spot where her blouse labors over a fold of skin that won't budge no matter how many crunches she does every morning.

Georgia averts her eyes as if she'd just walked in on Nikki giving me a blow job. Nikki blinks, almost as if I've cold-cocked her. She pauses for a second, and then looks right into my soul and replies in perfect body language, "You miserable sack of shit."

By the time Nikki cuts the first piece of lemon tart, I've polished off the rest of the Williams Selyem 2001 Chardonnay and my head is pounding. We've been chatting too politely, exhausting our topics of conversation: Emma and Sophie's summer plans, Washington bike paths, Georgia's film on Lewis and Clark, and Nikki's new fundraising client, a literacy group based in Northern Virginia.

Nikki fills the tea kettle and rummages in the pantry. "No tea. How can we enjoy our sweets and Stilton without tea?"

"I'll fetch you some," I offer, trying to be funny and a little mean, too. Mainly, I just need air.

"Take Hugo with you, Tad." Nikki looks at me like I'm a

stranger. I've really pissed her off. Took long enough.

The Coopersmith-Kornfelds can probably spare a tea bag. I knock on their door, not knowing what I'll do if Becca answers. Tell her that all her pole dancing is paying off? That I liked what I saw when I watched her unload her groceries the other day? Hugo needs to crap, which saves me from myself. I walk away quickly, not knowing if she even answers the door. I haven't played ding-dong-ditch since I was twelve.

I'm too drunk to drive anywhere, so I walk a mile to the 7-Eleven. They'll carry Lipton, which will have to do for the Brontë sisters, who are probably shredding me right now. Not that I don't deserve it. I'm a cad. I've become that underachieving Harvard guy whose arrogance unsuccessfully masks his "I got picked last for kickball" disappointment in life. I'm Charles Emerson Winston III, the Bostonian whom Alan Alda torments in old *M*A*S*H* episodes. My insignificance overwhelms me. A ball-breaker wife like Becca Coopersmith would have lassoed me, insisted that I pull myself together. Nikki used to be like that; I want that Nikki back.

Hugo leads me to the park around the corner from our cul-de-sac, where I throw a stick for him to retrieve while I sit on Sophie's favorite swing, dragging my feet. Dust smokes around my calves.

Georgia is gone by the time I return from the 7-Eleven with a box of Lipton tea bags. The dishwasher hums and a mound of soiled linen napkins lies on our kitchen table. I am sick with shame and loss, the loss of Georgia's reflection of who we were. That mirror broke tonight; its shards puncture my heart. In a vain attempt to rinse my mouth of the foul taste of the evening, I take a swig of Listerine. I let the khakis Nikki ironed drop on the bathroom floor. I stare at the tan lines from my sunglasses, at my flat eyes and newly chiseled cheekbones. I looked younger with a little baby fat.

I sidle up to Nikki, who lies coiled on her side of the bed. I close my eyes, willing the sunrise to come early, longing for my daughters to poke their heads in our room and wish us good morning. The girls haven't woken me up in a long time; I've been too busy swimming laps. Tomorrow I'll cook up a batch of blueberry pancakes. I'll try to make things right with Nikki. And then, for no reason, I'm angry again. And horny. I stroke the side of her face, and her tears wet my fingers. I still want to have enthusiastic sex. How did I get here?

I roll away from her, and through a bent slat in our blinds I study a cluster of spindly pines backlit by the moon. It seems like hours pass before the tension of the evening drains from my limbs. Just as I'm drifting off to sleep, Nikki yanks the warm sheets from my body. I shiver. She grabs my waist, rolls me over on my back, and mounts me. I can feel her nakedness on my belly. She grabs my hands and hoists them over my head. She's going to kiss me; we're going to have married sex nonpareil. In slow motion, she lowers her face toward me. She looks like she did when she pushed out Emma and Sophie: fierce, brave, fed up with the pain. Her hair is wild and her breath caresses my face; it smells like toothpaste and Stilton and alcohol. I want her. My lips part, waiting, waiting for her to kiss me. Her mouth comes within a millimeter of mine before she jerks her head away, slapping her hair against my face. She slides one hand from my wrists down toward my throat, and then she presses her dry lips to my jugular and growls.

GEORGIA AND PHIL
Georgia Dumfries, December 2003

Phil Scott shells pink pistachios at breakneck speed, leaving the detritus for Georgia to vacuum up later. The Redskins are winning 13-10, and the sportscaster's baritone blends with the hum of the dryer tumbling a load of Phil's whites. This afternoon the sound annoys Georgia. Without glancing up from her novel — she's reading *My Ántonia* for the fourth time — she knows the half is over by the feel of Phil's stained fingers rubbing the inside of her arm.

She puts down her book and leads him upstairs to her bedroom, where she'd made up the bed with a fresh pair of sheets (one thousand thread count) moments before his arrival. After he kisses her on the mouth, he removes her glasses. She opens the top drawer of her nightstand and hands him a condom. Six minutes later, spermicide trickles down her thighs.

"Did you go?" This is Phil's language for inquiring about her orgasm.

"Hmmm." In six minutes? At least he asks. Nikki is right; ugly men are better in bed. They have to try harder. Phil is better-looking and younger than Georgia; he calls on schedule,

wipes down the toilet basin after he pees, blogs about the con-
flict in Darfur, shoots the best video in town, and loops one of
his ropy arms around her torso after they make love. For the
past seven months, this weekly arrangement has been enough
for her. She turns her head into his sparse chest hair and
breathes in his scent: clove cigarettes and cat. Her nose starts
to tingle as if she's going to cry. God, she's been so needy since
her cat died. It's been almost seven months already.

Start to finish, they spend about fifteen minutes — roughly
the length of the halftime show — in bed. Georgia times it.
While she sprays Shout on the pink thumbprint he left on her
new sheets, Phil sneaks downstairs to catch the second half of
the game.

"Georgia?" he calls up to her in a sweet voice. "Mind taking
my clothes out of the dryer?"

Georgia does not yell. Ever. She walks down the two stairs
of her split-level condo in her terrycloth robe. "Got it." She
goes back up to her bathroom, washes herself, and puts on a
fresh pair of panties and the jeans and blouse she was wearing
earlier.

She slides her feet into slippers and pads over to the fridge.
"Hungry?" She also never uses more words than she needs.

"Always, after some good loving." Without looking away
from the game, he grins at her and reclines on the couch.

Georgia loves to cook. While retrieving two television trays
from her front hall closet, she muses about walking next week
to the All Soul's farmer's market across from the cathedral and
picking up a hearty bread and some butternut squash. She'll
buy fresh gingerroot and Asian pears from the vendor with the

bushy eyebrows, and come home and make a nice soup. Shopping and preparing a meal for Phil gives her Sundays structure, and the leftovers carry her through the week.

"You spoil me." He finishes his last bite of poached salmon and pats his stomach as lean people sometimes do to draw attention to their waistlines.

"You're right." The edge in her voice surprises her. Maybe she's going through menopause; her mother went through it in her early forties.

"You okay?"

For the first Sunday in seven months, she doesn't feel okay about their routine: cable television, bad sex, laundry, and a home-cooked meal, followed by the cell phone call on Wednesday afternoons. "I miss Willa." This is true, but it also lets Phil off the hook.

He pulls her toward him and strokes her hair. "How long were you two together?"

She likes the way he phrases the question. "Eleven years." Georgia and Phil initially bonded — they met a year ago when he sweet-talked her into editing his reel — over the respective pride in their cats' names: Mandu, to remind him of his travels to Kathmandu, and Willa Cat-Her, after her favorite author. Funny how such a simple exchange of information had led to their absurd coupling.

"Whoa. It's just going to take time." He kisses the top of her head. "It took about a year after my first kitty died before I was ready for another one. Now it feels like Mandu's been with me forever."

He strokes her hair again, wrapping a curl around his

pointer finger, and his tenderness embarrasses her. She extricates herself from him. "I've got an early day tomorrow." Tenderness is not part of the deal.

The next morning, Georgia awakens at five o'clock, unsettled from Phil's visit. Too agitated to sleep, she heads to the office to work in peace. She edits a scene for *The Mettle of a Marriage*, a reality television show that tests the strength of a seemingly happy marriage — an institution she rebuffed back in her thirties — by sending the husband or wife on a date with his or her first love.

Working on reality shows makes her feel greasy, but the day after she put Willa to sleep, she chipped a tooth and needed money to foot a hefty dentist bill. She began to suffer panic attacks over her meager savings and the prospect of growing old alone, so she swapped her earnest, broke public television colleagues for hungry young producers with hip haircuts.

She files her exchange with Phil in the back of her mind and parachutes into a stack of field tapes. Patient enough to mine footage for whispers and images, moments that would escape most editors' attention, she sculpts this material into perfectly rendered scenes. Today, she zeroes in on Wife Sheila hunting down a pair of miracle jeans that will hide what gravity has inflicted upon her rear end.

Heidi, her producer, breezes into the edit suite at nine-thirty with two skim lattes. Even though she's young, she has the look of a woman who has dated too many married men.

She hands Georgia the steaming cup. "So what have you got?" Georgia hits the space bar on her Avid, and the clip resumes playing.

When the sequence is over, Heidi whistles in genuine awe. "Fucking wizard, Georgia." She puts down her latte. "That shot of Sheila struggling with her waistband is killer. I totally missed that."

Georgia is disturbingly good at her job. Her editing prowess enables her to exploit this poor middle-aged woman, whose thighs look like her own, like someone stuffed a vat of cottage cheese into an old pair of pantyhose.

Heidi pulls up a chair and sits too close to Georgia. "I totally nailed that interview. What a boo-hooer! She was so into that high school flame. They like played in a band together or something. And her husband Joe is a marathon runner, he's probably Viagra-dependent from all that exercise." Heidi natters on while Georgia continues to shuttle through the footage, willing Heidi to stop talking. "Major flippage in store for this one," Heidi snorts.

Flippage is the network's term for the moment when the spouse moves from mild interest to obsession over his or her first love. Flippage makes fools out of perfectly normal people, makes them do crazy things. *Good job, Heidi. Congratulations on ruining another marriage.* "You sure know how to pick 'em," Georgia mutters.

Heidi, reeking of equal parts Camel Lights, Altoids, and Clinique Elixir, laugh-hacks as she wheels her chair closer to Georgia.

"Heidi, personal space."

"No problem." Because Heidi respects bitchiness, she moves to the producer's chair without argument.

Heidi flits in and out of the edit suite for the duration of the morning and brings Georgia a bowl of lentil soup and a warm slice of bread from the Greek deli for lunch. At five o'clock, her cell phone and Georgia's line ring simultaneously. Georgia does not own a cell phone. What would be the point? She's only received a dozen phone calls since she began working here, mostly short ones from Phil on Wednesdays during the early evening, while he walks to Chief Ike's for his weekly beer and pool game with his soundman, Eric Solonsky. Everyone loves Eric. He delivers the cleanest sound around. He's also Nikki's favorite neighbor. Small world.

"Hey there," Phil croons in a playful tone.

"Hi." Georgia puts her finger over her free ear to drown out Heidi's raspy laugh.

"Would anyone object to us having dinner tonight?" He shifts to his fake debonair persona.

Dinner? "What's up?" She shuttles through footage of Sheila enduring a bikini wax.

"Can't a guy take his girl for a meal?"

His girl? Phil's use of this pronoun gives her a start. It's the dead-endedness of her relationship with him, not his dimpled smile or compassion, that appeals to Georgia. But what the hell, it's just dinner. She agrees to meet him in half an hour and hangs up.

"I'm taking off early," Georgia announces to Heidi, who raises an eyebrow, removes her glasses, and folds her hands on her lap.

"Dinner plans."

"But there's more, ma chérie. Do tell." She does her best Catherine Deneuve.

Georgia considers telling Heidi about Phil; she doesn't have many girlfriends. Nikki meets her for dinner periodically, inhaling her meal without chewing, pretending that there's space in her life for more than raising her twins and helping Tad resuscitate his dead political career. Heidi is actually an articulate listener, which is why she's such a good interviewer. But confiding in Heidi, like polishing off a row of Thin Mints, would feel great while she's doing it and rotten immediately afterwards.

"I'll be in at eight tomorrow," she says and shuts down her computer.

Georgia follows a leggy hostess to an empty table at the Basil Café and downs two glasses of Merlot while waiting for Phil to arrive. A man in a leather jacket, spiky red hair, and a strong jawline glides past the hostess with a wink; he looks like Ed Norton. Phil.

"So sorry I'm late." He extends his hand, and when Georgia tries to shake it, he scratches his head. "Gotcha." And then he points his finger at her like he's shooting her and gives her arm a squeeze.

Why would anyone think it feels good to have the flesh of one's triceps pulled from the bone?

"Whatcha drinkin'?" He points to the wine glasses.

"I don't know, but it's good." She glances to the end of the

bar, at a handsome young man wearing a carefully coiffed ponytail and clogs.

"He sent you these?" Phil looks toward the man with
interest.

"Gotcha." She fake shoots him back.

"That's good. Very good." His eyes twinkle as he motions
to the waitress and orders a glass of port for himself. They
eat penne out of bowls the size of Frisbees while Phil describes some footage he's just shot of a baby for a film about
fetal alcohol syndrome. His passion charms Georgia, making
her ache to ditch Heidi and the lucratively boring side gigs
for the chance to work on a real film again. She wants to ask
why they're drinking too much wine in this Italian bistro on
a Monday night, just one day after their routine date, but she
doesn't. Georgia is good at waiting.

The air is balmy for a Washington winter night. Phil grabs
Georgia's hand as they walk from the restaurant to his English
basement apartment in Adams Morgan; she can't remember
the last time a man grabbed her hand. It feels good. His place
smells like the clove cigarettes he smokes on occasion and less
like cat pee than she had anticipated. She shrugs her sweater
off, aware that he's watching her.

"They're nice." He points at her breasts.

She can't wipe the goofy smile off her face. He lights a candle
and plays an old Joni Mitchell record. She likes Joni Mitchell.

Georgia looks around the apartmeßnt. "Where's Mandu?"

"She's shy." He disappears into his bedroom and returns

with a ginger tabby under his arm. "*Hewwo,* kitty cat. This is Georgia."

Beneath the baby talk, his voice is gentle. That uncomfortable feeling from the day before returns, but she wants to stay more than she wants to flee. She reaches for the silky fur beneath Mandu's chin and rubs the sweet spot until she purrs.

Phil nods. "She only likes special people."

Special people? How many women have met this cat? A pang of something like ownership surprises Georgia.

"Can I get you something to drink? A glass of vino maybe?"

"Sure." While he fusses with the corkscrew, she examines a framed black-and-white photo, Henri Cartier-Bresson–like in composition and feel. A little boy with a dirty nose and torn jeans stands amid a sea of broken glass and cigarette butts. He's holding a balloon. The lighting is perfection, and Phil's captured both the raw hope and flatness in the child's eyes. The image, like many of those she'd seen when editing Phil's reel, puts a lump in her throat.

"This is beautiful." Georgia points to the picture.

He looks at her like a puppy who's just received a biscuit. "Thanks."

He retrieves a wine glass from a cupboard, and she studies another photo hanging on the wall, a badly composed snapshot of a younger, goateed Phil with his arm slung around the shoulders of an older woman with enough freckles to suggest that her hair was once red like his. Must be his mother. "You two look alike," Georgia comments.

"She passed away five years ago."

Before Georgia can respond, he comes up behind her

and kisses her neck, leaving the slightest bit of moisture on her skin. He kneads her shoulders until the tension dissolves from her body. And a full hour later, when he asks her if she has "gone," she answers him truthfully with a yes. She drifts off with Phil's fingers resting on her wrist and Mandu's heat curling around her toes.

When Georgia wakes up the next morning, Phil is shaving in the bathroom, wearing a pair of boxers that she recognizes from doing his laundry.

"How'd you sleep, Georgia girl?" His voice is full of mischief. "You were something last night."

She buries her head under the covers, embarrassed by all her thrashing and thrusting.

He laughs. "Hey, listen, remember that shoot in Toronto I told you about last night?" He rinses thin lines of shaving cream from his cheeks. "Do you think you could take care of Mandu while I'm gone?"

"Yes." While stroking Mandu's stomach, she imagines leisurely Sunday mornings with Phil, reading the paper, sipping hot vanilla-flavored coffee, wiping butter and jam from the sides of each other's mouths. Or maybe they'd be like one of those freshly showered couples she endures when she breakfasts at Café Luna with her Sunday *New York Times*, the ones who laugh too hard at each other's jokes over their pancakes and eggs. *Think, Georgia, think.* What are you doing? Remember the stale jokes and the Metallica CD you spotted on his bookshelf. And don't forget last night, when the mushroom detritus on his chin made the waitress he'd been flirting with look away.

He finishes dressing and sits down next to her on his bed. "You're the sweetest. Sleep as long as you like, tiger." He cups her chin. "Roar."

She smiles. "Bye."

"You should do that more." He runs his finger over her lips. "Pretty."

She couldn't stop if she wanted to.

A vague sense of recognition orbits around her head as she tries to name the feeling that's taking hold of her. Holy shit. Flippage. She doesn't flip. She won't flip, like her mother and her sister, always waiting for some husband (seldom their own) to phone and say that he'd be ten minutes, twenty minutes, two hours late. Don't wait up for me, babe — the sure warning sign that he'd had his fill. Georgia has done an excellent job of insulating herself from this by dating men she doesn't really like, and she certainly isn't going to let anyone, even someone with a cat as fine as Mandu, come along and turn her into a heap of goo. No thanks.

She dials Heidi's cell phone to tell her that she'll be in late.

"Phil Scott?" Heidi teases. "He shot for me once." She whistles. "He's H-O-T, hot."

Georgia hates caller ID. "Just feeding a friend's cat, Heidi."

"You know that cute promotion producer, the Sheryl Crow look-alike? She had a huge, and I mean like rabbit-in-the-pot, stalker-huge thing for that guy."

"I'm just feeding his cat."

Phil offers no reason for extending his trip by ten days. While he's away, Georgia thinks about him on days other than Wednesday and Sunday, perhaps because she stops by his house every evening to play with Mandu. She visits her favorite pet store, buys organic catnip and a furry toy possum attached to a fishing pole, and runs around the living room dangling the possum, with Mandu in hot pursuit. She brushes Mandu's fur and strokes her while she drinks Phil's coffee and reads. She smiles for no reason and edits meandering scenes of special moments between Sheila and her husband. Heidi complains that she's lost her edge, that her sequences have become maudlin. She covers her gray with an auburn rinse, picks up a brochure for Lasik eye surgery on her way out of her optometrist's office, and buys a pair of pointy black shoes, the kind Heidi wears. She calls her sister and listens with interest while she describes her new boyfriend, Ned, who is so much more "present" than her last husband, Steve.

Phil is scheduled to return home on a Monday night. On Sunday afternoon, wearing her hip new shoes, Georgia visits her vendor with the bushy eyebrows. She buys eight beautiful pears; she'll bake Phil a tart. It's a cold winter day, and the air cuts through her coat and sweatshirt, hardening her nipples. Nice. She blushes, remembering Phil's comment about her breasts. During the cab ride to his apartment, she replays that night over in her head a million times.

She lets herself inside and stands in the entryway ready for Mandu to greet her, a ritual that has become the best part of her day. She listens for her meow, kneeling down, fingers poised for the touch of her smooth fur.

The phone rings. Georgia watches the little red light on the answering machine blink. "Hey, it's Eric. Not sure if you're back from Toronto. Let me know if you want to play on Wednesday." She's pleased that the voice does not belong to a woman. But why wouldn't he have taken Eric on the shoot? Eric always does his sound. It's probably a low-budget project. "Sorry again I couldn't help out with your cat. Hope that woman who does your laundry came through for you. Call me."

Blood rushes through Georgia's body, right through to the tips of her fingers. She sits down on Phil's couch dumbly. Mandu climbs on her lap and looks up at her with those steely gray eyes, as if she knows what an asshole her owner is, as if to say, "Thanks for the gourmet grub, but didn't I try to warn you?"

How could she have been so stupid? Flippage, schlippage. What a dunce. This is her punishment for ridiculing poor Wife Sheila and everyone else who has ever been naïve enough to participate in her slimy television show. Why did she have to tinker with her arrangement with Phil? Think that it could ever be more than it was? That a guy who could attract some Sheryl Crow look-alike would really be interested in her? That she could ever be more than the woman who does his laundry?

God, she's tired. She closes her eyes for a second, and she recognizes herself as the hungry, desperate little boy in the photo that so endeared Phil to her on that fateful night.

Forty-five minutes later, Mandu is licking her cheek. She reaches to stroke Mandu's arched back. What a cliché, a fortysomething spinster with a fierce attachment to a cat, whoring out her one real talent so she can store a few more pennies for her twilight years. Those golden years when her contemporaries will retire and travel cross-country in Winnebagos, or live off of their spouse's life insurance policies and Social Security checks. There will be no children to visit her in a nursing home when she's lost her teeth and hair and the wits to pee in a toilet.

It's dusk when she ventures outside for some air. The temperature has dropped, and her shirt, dampened from sleep, sticks to her body. She walks until the back of her heel grows hot with the promise of a blister. Her eyes burn, but she doesn't cry. Her limbs feel like rubber, but she doesn't slow down. She enters a gourmet deli and sees her crazed look reflected in the storekeeper's eyes; he quickly rings up a pound of hot-pink pistachio nuts.

She walks back to Phil's apartment and opens a bottle of his wine, hoping he was saving it for a special occasion. She's never been much of a smoker, but she lights up one of his cloves, coughing as the smoke moves down her throat. She sits on the couch and cracks the nuts open. She stuffs the meat into a baggie — she hates the taste of pistachios — leaving a mound of splintered shells on Phil's black carpet. She enters his bedroom, and with her stained fingers pinches his dirty polyester sheets into a pink tie-dyed pattern. "Come here, Mandu." She picks up the cat to say goodbye, truly her intention, but just as she leaves, just as she should release Mandu back into the empty apartment, she breaks into that goofy flippage smile as she shuts Phil's door behind her. She walks past the Basil Café and the darkened gourmet deli and her vendor's empty fruit stand. The hard leather of her shoe zests a layer of skin from her heel, but she ignores the warm blood trickling toward the sole of her foot. She just keeps moving. Her arms cradle Mandu to her breasts, shielding her against the cold breath of winter.

THE #42

Amy Solonsky, January 13, 2005

'm pregnant, not crippled," Amy says, refusing Leon's offer to ferry her from her office to her acupuncture appointment in Adams Morgan, her old neighborhood. She takes a swig of bottled water and shuts down her computer. She hears Leon's other line ring and hopes he'll pick up, but he doesn't. "I'll take the bus."

"Why?" Leon inquires. Unlike Amy, Leon has never lived in Washington, D.C., even when he was single. He prefers the accoutrements of their suburban life, the drive-through Starbucks and minty clean strip malls.

"I want someone to offer me a seat." She grins. "You know." She points to her swollen belly even though they're talking on the phone and he can't see her.

"You wanted to eat ice cream and pickles, too, and both made you sick," he reminds her.

"Guess I had to discover that for myself." Her tone is sharper than she intends.

Leon persists. "Honey, you're being ridiculous. I'll pick you up, and we can have an early dinner at that Italian hole in the wall you like."

Amy flinches. Installing the car seat, assembling the crib, taking an infant CPR class, these are activities they can do together. But Adams Morgan? No way. It belongs to another part of her life. It belongs to her.

"Okay, you're not backing down on this one." He laughs warmly. "It's actually kind of cute."

Oh, please. The fatter she gets, the cuter she becomes to Leon. "I'll see you at home at seven."

It's been so many years since Amy's taken the #42 that she doesn't even remember the price of a ticket. She drops three dollars in quarters into the fare box and surveys the crowded bus for a place to sit. With a shy smile, she wonders who will offer her a seat, but she's not the kind of pregnant woman who carries her baby like a neat little soccer ball glued to her pelvis; she just looks hefty. Not one passenger budges.

She grabs a pole for balance, trying to ignore the gummy substance that in turn sticks to her fingers. Some kind of hair gel, she guesses from the smell. She distracts herself with fantasies of spinach empanadas and plump cinnamon scones from Tryst. Maybe she'll treat herself to a nice cup of tea at Avignon Frères, her old hangover spot.

Two teenage girls wearing low-rise jeans and pointy shoes swap beefs about their mothers. "Like, she told me she could see my crack when I bent down, so she made me change my jeans before I left for school," the one with the nose ring groans. Amy recalls her sister's battles with their mother over piercing her ears. Hannah lost.

A woman with a long silver braid points to Amy's stomach and rises, gesturing to the empty seat she's vacated, "Please." A burning pain shoots down the back of Amy's thigh, so she nods in gratitude and takes the seat. She'll return to Adams Morgan every week if sticking needles in her body can offer some relief from this sciatica, yet another gestational malady.

Amy unbuttons Leon's pea coat and loosens her scarf. Why is she the only one sweating? She opens her compact and smothers a pimple with cover-up stick. Like, I'm thirteen again, she thinks. Someone is wearing Obsession; the sweet fragrance practically coats her tongue. She's turned into a bloodhound.

She feels guilty that she doesn't love being pregnant, like she's pissing on her good fortune, as her father would have said. She's been trying not to complain to Leon, who has waited years to start a family. The bus jerks to a stop, and she zips her compact into her purse.

It seems as though it's taking forever to get off the bus. The teenage girls are in front of Amy, complaining about their curfews now. Move it or lose it, she wants to say, I'm famished. And then, with no warning, her impatience balloons into anger: If you only knew how much it sucked to carry you guys, you'd grab a pen and write your mothers a thank-you card. Right now.

A waft of fresh air tempers her mood. Did they move Avignon Frères? Leaning closer to the window for a better view of Columbia Road, she doesn't see the abandoned algebra textbook at the top of the bus stairs until it's too late. "Jesus!"

she bellows as she falls on her rear end and bounces down two steps with her legs sticking straight out, like a child taking a ride down a banister. By the time she reaches the bottom, her skirt is gathered around her thighs, revealing the intersection of black knee-highs and unshaven white flesh. Her hands fly to her belly out of instinct, but when she replays her fall, she can't remember if her first concern was for the health of her baby or whether anyone had witnessed her tumble.

"Let me give you a hand." The bus driver bolts out of her seat to extend a thick forearm to Amy. "My balance was for shit when I was pregnant."

"Thanks." The scent of Obsession gushes from the driver's warm hand. Mystery solved. Amy puts her palm on her belly and wills the baby to move. The baby gives Amy a swift kick in the ribs, and her shoulders relax with the knowledge that all is A-okay inside the womb. Thank God. She tugs her skirt down over her knees, adjusts her glasses, and scans the faces of the passengers lined up outside the bus. Only one is stifling a giggle. Not bad. She herself is the type of person who would laugh nervously at such a wipeout.

It's a pretty day; the sky is blue, and four-o'clock shadows stripe the sidewalks of Columbia Road. Amy takes a big old Lamaze breath and waits for the walk signal. When she looks up, a man is standing on the other side of the crosswalk, leaning against the traffic-light pole, smiling at her. She recognizes him from the way he buries his thumb in his jeans pocket, jutting out his hip. His hair is thinner, but still spiky and red. Phil. The last guy she slept with before Leon. Crap.

He waits for her as she debates hopping back on the bus or yanking off a manhole cover and climbing in. Instead, she wraps Leon's coat around her belly and crosses the street.

"Grand entrance." His smile is kind.

He must have eaten garlic recently. "I try." In a futile effort to hide her blemish and her bulge, she looks down at the pavement. What the hell. She opens her coat, exposing herself to him like a flasher.

"Ah, I see."

Amy meets his eyes, still lovely. She's relieved to have revealed her condition. "Guess I'm officially off of the booty-call list."

He inches half a step closer, and she breathes in the sweet scent of his jacket: clove cigarettes and pot and leather. His breath grazes her forehead and makes her pores water, first under her armpits and then between her breasts. She wants her body back. She wants to stretch out on Phil's dirty sheets and run her hand over her abdomen, let her fingers linger on the jagged edge of her hipbone. She wants to relive the night they met, and the many that preceded and followed it. Nights of a thousand promises. She misses drinking Chianti at the Spaghetti Garden with Nadine. She misses stumbling down 18th Street to shoot pool at Chief Ike's, equally disgusted and flattered by the men who stared at her tight ass as she leaned over to break. And she misses her size-ten jeans. She longs to beckon a lungful of smoke into her cells — ones she doesn't have to share — to collect phone numbers from men she won't call, or to settle into an arrangement with a guy like Phil, a friendly fuck on a cold night.

Maybe, just for an hour, she can remove this baby from her womb, find a safe place where nothing will happen to it. And then, swear to God, she'll put it right back.

RIPE

Phil Scott, January 20, 2005

'm hungry. But that's not why I'm standing in front of the McDonald's on Columbia Road at 4:37 on a freezing cold Tuesday afternoon. I'm waiting for Amy Solonsky.

A week ago, I watched her fall on her heart-shaped ass trying to get off the #42. We hadn't seen each other in a couple of years, but I recognized her hair — miles of black curls — and her glasses with the tiny purple rectangular frames. Graphic artists sport hip eyewear as a rule.

I was standing across the street, so I couldn't help her up. She put her hand on her swollen belly right away and smiled with her eyes closed, as if she'd just heard some good news. She didn't notice me until she brushed off the tumble and was about to cross the street. I let her decide whether or not to come to me, and I was so glad that she did. "Phil," she said, and hearing my name coming out of her mouth moved me. Ever since I saw her, I've wanted something, but I don't know what it is, as if I'm kicking back on my couch after a grueling shoot, my bones aching, an ice cold beer in one hand, remote in the other, clicking and clicking, searching for a ball game, an old movie, a *Law and Order* rerun, anything that will unlatch me from myself.

It's 4:44. The bus is late. No surprise, it's D.C. I never had to wait for Amy before. She would always find me after one of her breakups, until she married a widower with an architecture firm in the 'burbs. Leroy or Leonard or something. She met him on the plane going to her father's funeral. I know this because my soundman Eric is Amy's brother.

At 4:48, a noticeably larger Amy treads carefully down the steps of the #42. Her coat won't button over her belly. She spots me and gives me her little amused smile as she waits for the Do Not Walk sign to turn.

When she's almost across the street, I say, "You need some company." I don't even know where she's going.

"And that would be you?" She adjusts her glasses.

"Why not?"

"I can think of a few reasons." She laughs.

We start walking down Columbia Road together like we've been in step our whole lives. She tells me that carrying the baby has given her sciatica, so she's been going to a prenatal acupuncturist on Belmont Road. She's a little short of breath, the way my sisters were when they were pregnant.

I follow her into an old brownstone, where she accepts a Dixie cup of peppermint tea from a receptionist with three diamond studs in her nose. The nurse calls her right away. Before she disappears through a door marked Patients Only, she turns around and smirks at me, and we swallow a laugh at the absurdity of us together right now, as if we're the only two people at a dinner party who just heard the hostess fart. The receptionist smiles at me, no doubt assuming I'm Amy's husband. I suppose I look like I might be somebody's husband; I'm a thirty-five-year-old guy with thinning hair and a niece soon to graduate from high school.

I read an article about the lies mothers tell their children in *Brain Child: The Thinking Mother's Magazine* and listen to my stomach howl, which reminds me of the long, hungry stakeouts I endured when I was cutting my teeth shooting local news. Thank God those days are over.

An hour later, Amy emerges. Her hair is messy and her eyes are glassy, like she's just had some killer weed or gotten her brains fucked out. Amy loves to fuck. She walks toward me, her belly sticking out of a red jersey with black buttons, each one a different shape. Her tits are swollen up to twice their normal size.

"Look, Phil," she says, "I can move again." She raises her hands over her head and wiggles her hips. "I could even merengue if I wanted to."

The receptionist winks at her. "Let's not get too carried away, Britney Spears."

Amy slings her coat over her arm, and we walk out into the cold.

"Aren't you freezing?" I ask, my breath coming out of my mouth like smoke.

She shakes her head no. I don't want to kill her buzz, so I just follow her to the Spaghetti Garden.

She nods her head toward the restaurant. "I forgot my wallet."

I reply by opening the door for her. She leads me to a small table at the back.

"You're supposed to drink lots of water," I instruct her. I'd only heard the receptionist say this about nine times. "And speaking of which, I'll be back in a second."

"I'll order an appetizer," Amy says.

I piss, thinking about what we might talk about when I return to the table. We could reminisce about the day we met, at Eric's son's bris, and how we were so freaked out by the ceremony that afterwards we split a pitcher of sangria at El Tamarindo, and how easy it was to fall into bed six months later when we ran into each other shooting pool at Chief Ike's. We could gossip about Eric and Maggie or producers we hate. We could lament the fucked-up war in Iraq. We'll talk of none of these things, I predict.

Amy's putting her cell phone back into her purse when I approach the table. I don't ask who was on the phone, and she doesn't tell me. A few minutes later, the waiter brings her a steaming plate of fried calamari, and she digs in. I take a bite of garlic bread. The butter is still cold, but I'm so hungry that I wolf down three slabs anyway.

Amy and I eat in perfect time. Bite. Chew. Gulp. She's licking her fingers when our skinny, androgynous waiter, who must live in Adams Morgan because I recognize him from Tryst, comes to take our dinner order.

"That was fantastic. I'd like a bowl of pasta puttanesca and a ginger ale," she says. "Oh, and some more bread please."

He raises a pierced eyebrow.

I'm full but not satisfied, so I order a bowl of pasta. It's tastier than the garlic bread, but now I'm too stuffed to eat much of it. Amy and I never had much to say to one another when we weren't shooting pool or in bed, so we eat in near silence like an old married couple. I pay the bill.

Amy's nose is red from the cold, but she still doesn't put on her coat. She pops a mint into her mouth. I'm dying for a cigarette, but out of respect for Amy's condition, I hold off.

"I really want an ice cream cone, but that would be obscene." She laughs. I laugh at her laugh, which sounds like Horshack's in those *Welcome Back, Kotter* reruns I watch when I can't sleep. Not what you'd expect from someone so cool, and it's not just the eyewear. She's Amy, and she apologizes for nothing, not her ass, which some women might find too big, and not her eyes, which are a little too close together. Somehow you put it all together — the hair, the smile, the spunk — and it works.

I take her elbow and guide her into Ben and Jerry's. It's the first time we've touched since I saw her. A charge runs through my fingers, but not a horny charge. Strange. I watch her polish off a strawberry ice cream waffle cone with gusto.

"I miss my old 'hood," she admits wistfully. "I feel so free here." She takes a big breath and then sticks her hands on her belly, which ripples slightly under her shirt. I don't ask to feel the baby kick even though I want to.

It doesn't seem that strange to follow her down the steps to my basement apartment. I catch her scent, kind of citrusy, different from what she used to smell like. Usually when I'm bringing a woman home, I'm mapping out the night — do I have wine? pot? rubbers? Now I'm only thinking that I'm not thinking about that at all.

"Where's Mandu?" Amy asks.

I don't want to go there. I flew up to Ontario once to enjoy the foliage with a co-ed I'd met while shooting a marketing tape for a summer camp. When I came home, Georgia, the cat sitter and a woman I'd been seeing, told me she'd left a window open by accident.

"Gone," I say. I try not to think about how much I miss that cat.

She looks at me with sympathy, plops down on my couch, and sticks her feet on my coffee table while I rifle through my CDs. She giggles. "No Joni tonight."

"Was it that obvious?" I've always thought I should write Joni Mitchell a big thank-you note for getting me laid so often. For some reason, the kind of chick who digs Joni Mitchell digs me.

"Sort of," she replies in a "No shit, Sherlock" tone.

"What do you want to hear?"

"The street. I want to hear sirens and drunken laughter and Spanish." She brushes her hair off her face. "My neighborhood is so quiet it's creepy."

I open my window a crack, and lo and behold a police car rages by. "For you." I nod toward the street.

She points to a photo I took of a scruffy little boy holding a balloon. "You shooting stills these days?"

I like that she doesn't ask if I'm shooting weddings. People in the film biz are so fucking snobby about that. I started doing weddings for the extra cash, to help my oldest sister out of a bad marriage, but now I do it because I love shooting by myself, without any producer getting in my shit.

I pull out a stack of photos I shot a few weeks ago. Amy examines an image of the loneliest-looking woman I've ever seen: a barefoot waif wearing pearls and a bad bridesmaid's dress, looping her sandal straps around her pinkie, smiling at the bride who's wiping frosting from the groom's mustache.

"You're a savant, you know that? I can feel the woman's hollowness."

Amy's a good graphic artist, and I respect her eye. "Yeah, call me Rain Man." I try not to smile too hard.

She points to the thin woman in pearls. "Naked emotion."

"I smoked a clove with her after I shot that photo. She had this way of looking at you, aloof, yet like you could be the answer to her next prayer."

"What was her name?"

"Molly Flanders," I say wistfully.

"Send Molly Flanders this photo." Amy taps the picture with her fingers, so swollen that little folds of flesh bulge around her wedding ring, a thick silver band. She's not the type to sport the big rock.

And then what? I can't see fucking someone I've shot like that; it would be like mixing files. No. Definitely no. I don't reply.

"Really, Phil, send it."

Amy gets up and walks toward my bedroom, saying over her shoulder, "Come on, take my picture." I grab my camera bag and follow her. I'll go natural with this, just the moon and the street light.

She sits on my bed with her elbows resting on her knees and her face in her hands, and looks up at me unsmiling. After I snap the first picture, I'm home again. I anticipate what she's going to do, and I'm there before she does it. It's as natural to me as breathing or shitting.

I'm not surprised when she takes off her blouse and unhooks her bra. Blue veins zigzag up and down her breasts, which are so ripe I want to squeeze them as I would a grapefruit at the market. Her nipples look larger and browner than I remember, and her belly is round and taut. She slips out of her skirt and pulls off these black tights that come up to her knees. Her pink panties have lost their elasticity, and she tugs them down over her ass. I'd forgotten how beautiful she is.

She turns her back to me, raises her hands over her head, and moves her hips the way she did in the doctor's office. I shoot her from the side, hands on belly, head back, hair swimming down her spine. I shoot her front on, staring down my lens. I shoot and shoot until I run out of film.

When I finish, we collapse on my bed, spent. I lie as still as I ever have and listen to her breathe. She moves, accidentally grazing my bicep with her breast. I don't budge; I want us to stay precisely as we are. She sits up and dresses and kisses me on the cheek. We're done.

Outside, as I hail her a cab, she leans over to me so close that I can smell strawberry ice cream and calamari on her breath.

I think she's going to kiss me again, but instead she says, "Do you have any cash?" I give her my last bill, a fifty, more than enough to return her to the 'burbs.

The wind tears through my jacket right to my bones. I finally light up that clove, drawing the sweet smoke into my body, and watch Amy's cab until it rounds the corner. Across the street, a bottle breaks and a young woman laughs. If I listen hard, I can hear a siren off in the distance. I wonder if Amy hears it too.

JANUARY

Leon Falk, January 21, 2005

L ast night I stole my wife's wallet. I'm forty-five years old, and I've never taken so much as a loose grape from my grocery cart without paying for it. A half-pound of stuffed red leather, the contents of which could wreck my marriage, now weighs down the breast pocket of my parka, grazing my heart with my every move.

Still, I feel only a tinge of guilt that Amy is probably canceling her credit cards while I stand in her brother's kitchen cupping a warm Starbucks — straight black. I watch Eric's lips move as if he's the adult to my Charlie Brown. Wah, wah, wah. I've been renovating houses long enough to know that Eric and Maggie want more living space, a view of whatever will bloom in their garden this spring, and a bigger pantry.

"You look stressed, Leon."

I try to smile. "Oh, I'm all right, Eric."

"The Solonsky women can be 'bitchy breeders,' to quote Hannah. Amy been giving you a hard time?"

I'm tempted to tell him everything, that I showed up at Amy's office to drive her to her doctor's appointment even though I knew I'd been smothering her lately, that I found her wallet on her desk, that I tracked her down in Adams Morgan to give it to her, that I wished to hell I hadn't seen what I had.

"You with me?" Eric touches my sleeve.

His hand, inches from the wallet, makes me flinch. I assure him that I'm fine, and he tells me to lock up after I finish taking my measurements.

"You have a shoot today?" I want to know if he's meeting up with Phil. I want to know a lot more than that, but it's not right to badger Eric.

"Nope, errand day," Eric says.

I wish him a nice day or something feeble like that and stand slack-jawed in his kitchen, watching his Subaru drive down the hill, past the charming but small homes whose owners will call the Solonskys for a contractor referral come barbecue season, after they've filed into his house to inspect my work.

I haven't eaten since yesterday. I'm woozy. Now I've not only stolen my wife's wallet, I've swiped an apple juice box and a bag of multigrain Goldfish crackers from Eric and Maggie's soon-to-be-expanded pantry. I plunk down on the family room sofa, gobbling up cheddared cardboard, contemplating their photo albums lined up on the bookcase.

I succumb to my curiosity. I know Amy met what's-his-face at Alec's bris, so I pluck a family album labeled "Solonsky progeny." Bingo. I find a snapshot of Amy, Hannah, and their mother, who's holding Alec. Maggie has on a hippie-looking dress that she'd never wear now that she's "clinging to her fading soap-star looks," to quote Amy. Amy had short hair then, but it looks okay — shows off her eyes, so big that those little glasses she wears barely cover them. I like her hair long, though. It spills halfway down her back, and on lazy Saturday mornings I wash it for her, and my hands smell like her for the rest of the day.

I find *him* at the back of another album in a photo from a surprise thirtieth birthday party Hannah threw for Eric. Skinny redheaded weasel. Phil. He's sitting in an Adirondack chair at dusk, legs crossed, smoking a cigarette; it's a moody picture. He looks like the kind of guy you tell your sister to avoid. Amy told me about him early on, during one of those romantic history conversations I could have done without. I've slept with barely a handful of women. Amy. My late first wife, Mary, who was also my high school and college sweetheart. The olive-skinned lifeguard who helped me pass the summer after I graduated from college when Mary decided we needed to play the field. Oh, and some drunken sympathy sex from my bookkeeper in the back of her Toyota Sequoia during my first Christmas without Mary. My sexual history. Amy's feels more vivid to me.

What the hell was she doing with that guy last night? I would have felt better if they were talking or even laughing, but they were walking down the street in the familiarity of silence. Ridiculous. Just last week we were picking out baby names.

I slide off my parka, and the wallet thuds against the couch. My heart is pumping fast. I better hit the head. I need to get the hell away from this album and the wallet. Standing up too quickly, I step on the bag of Goldfish and relish the sound of the crackers crumbling under my boot.

Professional photos of Alec and Kaya line the hallway leading into the bathroom: various arrangements of the grinning kids whom Amy adores. I wash my hands and face with cold water. Feels good.

I start to dial Amy. She'll clear this up. She'll tell me that she bumped into Phil, that they were simply walking in the same direction, and then she ran into her friend Nadine, who treated her to dinner and ice cream — I found a crumpled Ben and Jerry's napkin in her coat pocket — and the forty-dollar cab ride from the city back to our house, a mile up the road from here. I'll apologize for hovering and acknowledge her need for time to herself, and tonight she'll cuddle up against me and remind me that I get weird in January, and we'll laugh about it all. I love Amy's laugh: half cackle, half bleat. My body relaxes, then tenses again from my skull down to my toes.

I have never squatted in a client's home. I grab my coat and pull out the wallet, still warm from my body, and go upstairs to scout the perfect spot to examine my spoils. First stop, Kaya's room. I'm not going to sit on her bed. Bad idea. A computer occupies much of her desk, the rest of which she's plastered with stickers of shiny teen idols with girlie haircuts. Next stop, Alec's room; his bed is perfectly made, baseball trophies line his shelves. He's not a good athlete, but according to Amy, these days you get some hardware for filling out a registration form. I don't pry into Eric and Maggie's bedroom.

Back downstairs, I decide on the kitchen table. I clear

away this morning's *Washington Post* and a cookbook opened
to a recipe for tomato soup, and then I take a sponge and wipe
three globs of jelly off the white surface. I dry it with a paper
towel and place the wallet right in front of me.

My hands are shaking. When the phone rings, I practically
shoot out of my chair like a pebble from a slingshot. The Goldfish are swimming up to my throat, every nerve in my body is
vibrating, and I'm not sure this is a bad thing. In ten years of
marriage to Mary, I never felt this scared or alive. When she
died, I was overcome with a dull ache that I can still evoke if I
stare too long at one of the few pictures of her I've kept, or if
I catch a whiff of Vaseline Intensive Care, the kind that comes
in the mint green bottle. Last year Amy dragged me to one of
those sappy female movies, and I thought I heard Mary weeping two rows back. I didn't turn around, but my heart stayed
heavy through the pizza and sex that followed.

I touch the bumpy red leather. It's a big wallet with room
enough for a change purse, a checkbook, a calendar, and a plastic case for credit cards. I open the case first. Visa, Maryland
driver's license, Washington Sport and Health, Blockbuster,
Aetna. I sort her forty dollars by denomination — a twenty, a
ten, and two fives. Bringing order to her things gives me a slender sense of peace and the courage to look at her calendar.

My upper lip starts to twitch as I flip through it. Surpris-
ing that a graphic artist, someone who works with computers
all day, would spurn a Blackberry, but Amy says she likes to
see the whole month on one page. It's late January, so I can see
only a few weeks' worth of past appointments and dates. I hate
January.

Sunday, January 4. Dinner with Eric and Maggie to discuss my ideas for their house. Eric made a hearty beef stew — red, the color of Amy's wallet. We dunked thick slabs of bread into our bowls, and I looked around the first floor musing about its possibilities. On the drive home, Amy squeezed my hand and told me that she likes my ability to see what's not there. Was she trying to tell me that I was missing something happening right under my nose?

Tuesday, January 6, 13, and 20. Three late-afternoon appointments to treat her sciatica at the Women's Acupuncture Center on Belmont and Columbia, Amy's old neighborhood. I know she has client meetings on Tuesdays, and she came right home after the first two appointments. She couldn't have seen Phil. I scour the squares for some code name for her secret lover, but I recognize all the names, and thank God, Phil's isn't one of them.

Friday, January 23. Blank. The anniversary of Mary's death.

I'm breathing easier now, but I'm still not satisfied that there aren't items in this wallet that might bite me. The house is so still that all I can hear is the hum of the fish tank, and then the sound of my hand unzipping the back compartment of the wallet. I take a deep breath before sticking my fingers into the small fold, where I find an airplane ticket stub. A memento of something. Maybe a trip she took with Phil to one of her conventions. Sweat trickles down my side, over the lump of flesh that I blame on Amy's recent potato chip habit. I turn the ticket over. Midwest Express. May 2001. If I close my eyes, I can see us on that plane where we first met: Amy sitting beside me in her funeral clothes, her eyes puffy and red, her fingers thankfully ringless, a dark-green bra strap sliding down her lovely shoulder as she told me about her father's unexpected death and the lake house they'd rented for their family reunion. Her father's heart attack, sudden and lethal, reminded me of Mary's aneurysm, so I tried to distract myself with a fantasy of Amy and me sitting in a fishing boat, face to face on that big blue lake, listening for a lucky splash. I cling to that moment and to the ones that followed, and to the ones ahead of us, which I no longer presume to plan or believe in despite Amy's constant reassurances that she's healthy.

I recognize the second piece of paper in the compartment. I lay the flimsy square on the table. This is Simon. We're going to name him after Amy's father. She could only open her heart to him after we met, after he was gone, she claims, although I don't understand why. The blurry white looks like a spider web superimposed on a black chalkboard. I can see only his profile, but Amy insists that he has my forehead and nose. The sonographer agreed, and they're not supposed to say things like that. Now that he's getting bigger, he can't fit into the frame. Amy and I are supposed to go for her twenty-four week sonogram next Thursday. She'll need her Aetna card.

I bring the image of Simon to my lips, gingerly fold the paper in half, and slide it back into the wallet. I want to see Amy, to kiss her neck and rest my fingers on her belly and wait for our son to move. In my haste to put miles between this morning and my wish, I reach for the ticket stub, knocking over my Starbucks cup. The cold coffee spills onto Amy's calendar, still splayed to reveal every week of January. I stop the flow with my sleeve, but half the dates, including yesterday's, are soaked. The ink has bled, making Amy's script illegible. The empty square marking the anniversary of Mary's death remains unsullied, as do the sonogram appointment at the end of the month and all the days thereafter.

MOLLY FLANDERS
Molly Flanders, Summer 2006

The night Molly met Becca Coopersmith, it rained so hard that it sounded like someone was pelting her skylight with marbles. She seduced her husband, Phil, his keys in hand, ready to drive to Chincoteague to shoot a film about the pony swim. Half naked, limbs intertwined, sweaty and breathless, they lay on the living room floor of their new house, where she clung to him like a war bride, more needy than embarrassed by her terror of thunderstorms and her dread of spending their first night apart. "I'll call as soon as I get there," he promised, zipping up his jeans.

A cold loneliness overtook Molly. Phil had been the only person to see inside of her. When he'd sent her a photo he'd taken of her at a wedding reception, she felt as though he'd understood her emptiness. She knew right then and there that she'd marry him. But because Phil could see the holes in her, it didn't mean that he could fill them, not even when he was inside her. Every time he took out his camera, she hoped he'd snap another photo that would expose another flash of her essence.

Molly got dressed and settled on the couch to compose a thank-you note to her aunt Katherine for a place setting of wedding silver. She heard a loud boom, and then the room went black and the howl of hot summer winds replaced the hum of the air conditioner. Her first power outage alone. With each clap of thunder, she imagined a new structural defect plaguing their house. Danny Weiss, her realtor, who was related to half the people on this cul-de-sac, assured her that the house was solidly constructed.

She couldn't remember which box contained their flashlights and candles, and the only neighbors she knew, Phil's soundman Eric and his family, were out of town. They'd promised to throw a party for Molly and Phil to welcome them to the neighborhood.

The steady crackle of lightning further unmoored Molly as she sat on the couch contemplating the slender light flickering in the window of the cute house across the street. Strong winds shook the branches of the enormous oak tree in the neighbors' front yard, rocking the swing where she'd spied one of their sons kissing his girlfriend the night before. When she could no longer tolerate the dark — even Hugo, the oversized, obnoxious dog next door, was barking in fear — she slipped on Phil's rain jacket and mustered up the courage to walk the thirty yards to the front steps of their neighbors' house.

She was just about to ring the bell when, through the screen door, she heard a woman chanting an ancient-sounding melody in a minor key. The guttural consonants, the gentle wailing, and the emotion embedded in every note transported Molly back twenty years to Nancy Cohen's bat mitzvah: to the packed sanctuary where her friend recited with authority from a large scroll; to the rabbi blessing Nancy, his eyes closed, his fingertips resting on her newly straight hair; to the hora and Hava Negilah; to the toasts and the tears and the joy. She'd felt so purposeless compared to Nancy. Her parents had always told her that being a Flanders heir meant something. But what? What could possibly mean more than having a bat mitzvah?

"How was I, baby?" the woman called out, her speaking voice much huskier than her singing one.

"You're still doing a little of the Joni Mitchell *Blue* thing," a male voice responded in a teasing tone.

Molly smiled. She wasn't much of a Joni Mitchell fan. Phil owned *Blue* on vinyl; he'd played it for her once early in their courtship, and she could indeed detect a bit of Joni in the woman's chant as she stood on that soggy porch, flooded with her old ache to share Nancy's heritage. Molly rang the bell firmly.

The woman appeared in the doorway carrying a fat purple candle that illuminated her strong cheekbones and jaw. She wore an ice-blue tank top and a choker, the beaded kind that hinted at exotic travels. She was one of those women who knew instinctively how to draw attention to her best features — in her case, her smooth, olive skin and pretty neck.

"Oh my God, come in. You just moved in, right? It's awful out there. Have you been sitting in the dark?" She clucked.

Molly felt foolish about how long it had taken to talk herself into walking across the street. "Sorry to bother you. I came to ask if I could borrow some candles or a flashlight."

"Come, come." The woman placed a warm hand on the small of Molly's back and escorted her into the musky-smelling living room. "I'm Becca Coopersmith." She smiled, revealing a dimple that could house a whole dime.

"Molly Flanders." Molly smiled back.

"My husband, Adam Kornfeld." Becca nodded to a man not much taller than she was, with thick brownish-gray hair and a ready smile. He wore jean shorts and a faded T-shirt bearing a Bowdoin College insignia that was beginning to crack.

By the time Molly removed her jacket, she'd learned that Becca's son Jason had become a vegetarian because of his extreme compassion for chickens, that her husband had just won an award for a social marketing campaign on recycling, that she had just started a new job as development consultant for a community health center, and that she grew her own greens because "everyone labels their produce organic these days."

"Your basement is going to be a mess." Adam had an authoritative yet cordial voice. "Give me your key. I'll bail you out."

She was a little flustered by his kindness, but she handed him her key anyway. "Are you sure?" she asked, her question followed by a loud crash from outside, where a sturdy branch had fallen from a tree, barely missing the hood of her Volkswagen. She wished Phil wasn't driving in the storm.

Becca gave Molly's shoulder a squeeze. "It's a mitzvah." She smiled. "A good deed."

Molly wasn't used to people doing nice things for her unless she paid them. "Thank you."

"Go." Becca kissed Adam on the cheek and turned back to Molly.

"What a lovely piece." Molly pointed to a wooden sculpture

of a mother holding her baby to her breast.

Becca stroked the mother's arm. "Olive wood. We got it in Jerusalem when I was pregnant with Isaac."

"Beautiful." Like the mezuzah necklace Nancy's Israeli uncle gave her for her bat mitzvah. These memories of Nancy kept showing up like unwelcome houseguests, but Molly was far too happy with her life, with her Phil, to fret about her old, fierce spiritual yearnings.

Becca removed her hand from the sculpture and waved Molly into the kitchen. "Let's eat ice cream by candlelight." She winked.

Molly was sure that Becca was a wonderful mother, the type who could make a trip to the post office seem like a grand adventure. She fantasized about one day baking Christmas cookies with her toddler. No maid would swoop in to erase their messes. She inspected the distressed farm table where Becca had set a candle that cast a warm light on a vase of blue hydrangeas. Molly imagined that the Coopersmith-Kornfeld family had spent many a meal there teasing each other or fighting over the last tofu burger.

Becca plucked a carton of carob-chip ice cream from her freezer. "I really shouldn't get near this stuff." She patted her hips, camouflaged by a long black peasant skirt that barely covered a tattoo of a dove on her ankle.

Molly just nodded. She'd inherited the metabolism of a hummingbird. "I like these bowls." They reminded her of the set she had shipped from Spain during her honeymoon.

"Pier One. I think they were three or four dollars apiece."

"They always have such great sales." Molly hadn't made

this kind of remark in a while, the kind that suggested that she had to cut corners like everyone else.

Becca placed a heaping bowl of ice cream in front of her and sat down with her own. "So tell me about you. What do you do to keep yourself busy?"

Molly was proud of the micro-enterprise programs she managed for the Flanders Philanthropic Fund, the result of long hours with little support from the foundation, but Becca was a fundraiser, and she didn't want to open up that discussion. Once people found out that you had family money, they assumed that you hadn't earned anything for yourself and started treating you with disdain, combined with just enough warmth to hit you up for something.

Before she could answer, Becca removed the spoon from her lips, closed her eyes, and let out a moan. "I need a cigarette." She moaned again. "Too bad I quit."

Molly laughed. It would be so easy to befriend Becca; she was just like Nancy, so funny and open and sure of who she was. They even shared the same dimple. God, she could practically feel Nancy with her in the room.

The rain started to slow down as Molly listened to Becca describe her sons' letters about their Outward Bound adventures and confide how unsettling yet relaxing she found the new quiet of her house.

"You're too good a listener, Molly." She reached for a bottle of red wine on the table and pulled out the cork. They were on their second glass of wine when Molly got up the guts to ask about Becca's chanting.

"I had an adult bat mitzvah a few years ago, and every year,

I read my Torah portion on the anniversary of the date."

"Adult bat mitzvah?" Molly's stomach tightened almost imperceptibly.

"I figured you weren't Jewish." Becca smiled warmly.

"I went to a bat mitzvah once. My best friend in elementary school was Jewish," Molly offered, perhaps a bit too eagerly. "Nancy Cohen."

"I never had one, so I wanted to have this moment with God."

Molly didn't know how to respond; she couldn't remember the last time she'd discussed anyone's religion, much less so casually.

"This is something I do for myself."

With no warning, Molly began to feel a humming in her body, the precursor to the pins and needles that had invaded her skin right before she'd reached into Nancy's jewelry box. She held the cool silver of the mezuzah chain in her hand while Nancy waited for her to come watch *The Partridge Family* with her Israeli cousins in the den.

"I hate to talk about it, because I probably sound like I've joined a cult or something." Becca wiped a carob chip from the table.

"Oh, no. Please go on. I'm fascinated." Molly was more than fascinated. She couldn't tear herself away from Becca's talk of the bat mitzvah, just as she couldn't stop biting her nails or cracking her knuckles. She felt like she was thirteen years old again, sitting in a red upholstered chair, trying to ignore the way her new pantyhose constricted her breathing, wishing she was up on that altar thanking her grandma Esther for flying in from Miami for her special day. The tingling was rising now, teetering on the verge of becoming that itch, the sensation distant and familiar at the same time. Goddammit. Not now, not Becca.

Adam appeared in the kitchen. Talk about divine intervention! Maybe the tingling would go away if Becca just stopped talking about her bat mitzvah.

Adam wiped a line of sweat from his forehead with the sleeve of his T-shirt. "When the power comes back, I'll bring over a few fans to dry the edges of your carpet."

Molly took care not to make Adam feel like he was her hired help, to sound gracious and avoid what Phil called her "master of the servants" tone. "Thank you so much for everything. You must have saved us hundreds of dollars."

He grinned. "Glad to help. I'm going to hose off."

"Thanks, Adam." She knew she should leave, but instead she took a big breath and begged Becca to tell her more about her bat mitzvah.

"Okay, but I get emotional when I talk about this one part."

"Now you *have* to tell me about it." Molly wanted to dig her nails into every square inch of her skin.

"Do you know what a tallis is?" Becca didn't wait for Molly to answer. "You know those prayer shawls you see people wearing around their shoulders?"

"Yes, they're beautiful." Even the insides of her ears were beginning to itch.

"Adam asked my mother to give him my grandfather's tallis from his bar mitzvah back in the old country. Lithuania." Her face began to flush. "So the night before the kids left for camp, we all went out to celebrate my forty-fifth birthday. Right after I blew out the candle on my raspberry mousse, Adam handed me this package he'd wrapped in lavender tissue paper, decorated by Isaac, the artist in the family. I opened it, and there was my grandfather's tallis — I recognized it right away." Tears flooded her little eyes.

Becca was assailing Molly with the meaning in her life, admittedly at Molly's request, but still. "How incredible that must have been for you!" Molly clenched her hands in her lap so she wouldn't scratch.

Becca wiped her eyes with a dish towel and sniffled. "God, this is so embarrassing!" She disappeared into the living room and returned with a navy blue velvet case embroidered with gold Hebrew letters. She removed the long, rectangular piece of fabric gingerly from the bag. It smelled musty. She combed her fingers through the fringes of the shawl. "When I wear this, I can practically feel generations of Jews passing right through my soul. I can feel God." She shuddered, folding up the tallis and returning it carefully to the bag.

How could this be happening? Molly thought she'd grown out of her Nancy envy, as she had her excessive use of the word "like." But here she was, yearning for what belonged to Nancy and Becca: grandparents who'd escaped pogroms, intense friendships formed at Jewish summer camps, a compulsion to complain about constipation from eating too much matzoh on Passover. She wanted Becca's highly compassionate sons, she wanted the adult bat mitzvah; she even coveted Becca's big rear end. She felt so beige, so meager. It wasn't as if she hadn't tried to replicate Nancy's spiritual abundance. In college, she joined a Quaker group. She hated it, and it wasn't just because of the mouth-breather who sat next to her. She'd grown up in a home with enough silence to last a lifetime.

"Becca?" Adam called from the top of the steps. "Can you bring me another flashlight? My battery died."

Molly took deep breaths and rubbed her palms together.

"Just a sec," Becca hollered back. Jewish people liked to talk to each other from different rooms, Molly remembered from Nancy's family. She watched Becca hunt around in her junk drawer for another flashlight and run upstairs.

Molly sat alone with the tallis and her empty Pier One ice cream bowl, burning with that godawful lust. The rain had tapered off into a light drizzle, punctuated by the occasional gush of water from Becca's downspouts. She took the worn tallis out of its bag and held it against her face; she wanted it even more than Nancy's mezuzah or the picture of Mr. Cohen stuffing a wadded-up piece of paper into the Wailing Wall. Anything else she'd ever wanted in her life — clothes, vacations, sometimes even friends — she'd simply bought for herself.

The floorboards creaked above her head, and she prayed that Becca would fly down the stairs in time to save her from herself. More whispering and giggling. She ran her fingers along the creases of the tallis, put it in the large inside pocket of Phil's jacket, and stuffed a folded dish towel into the velvet case.

Becca reappeared in the kitchen, and they talked for a few more minutes.

"I better head home," Molly said through a yawn.

Becca gave her a flashlight and a week's supply of batteries.

"Should I walk you?"

"It's just across the street. Don't be silly. Please thank Adam."

"Hug." Becca pulled her in close.

When Molly hung Phil's jacket in the bathroom, a few raindrops slid off the Gortex and tickled her feet. She cradled the tallis to her body. Flashlight in hand, she retrieved a knife from the kitchen and an unopened moving box labeled Trust Documents from the messy study. She punctured the packing tape, running the knife along the seam of the box, entirely certain about where she'd packed her valuables.

She slid her hand beneath a college notebook filled with aborted feelings, a packet of old love letters, some loose photos of her ex-boyfriend, and felt the soft velvet jewelry pouch against her fingers. She loosened its gold drawstrings and withdrew Nancy Cohen's tarnished silver mezuzah.

She returned to exactly where she'd been sitting earlier that evening while she contemplated walking over to Becca's house. The mezuzah kissed the skin a couple of inches below her collarbones, and the flimsy satin of the tallis felt cool against her shoulders. Humming the melody she'd heard Nancy and Becca chant, she ran one hand through the silky fringes of the prayer shawl and fingered the mezuzah with the other. Her skin no longer itched.

The storm passed, and Becca's house lit up. Hugo had finally stopped barking. Molly made no move to turn on the air conditioning, because she didn't mind the heat; she didn't

reset the phone, because she didn't know what she'd do if
Becca called. She put Phil's copy of *Blue* on the turntable and
listened for the scratches, the trilling, the echoes of gentle
wails.

MINOCQUA BATS

Becca Coopersmith, September 2006

On a Tuesday morning in September, Becca Coopersmith pressed the only black suit she owned. She hadn't
touched an iron in years. The cab would be here in an
hour to ferry her to Reagan National, where she'd catch a flight
to Rhinelander, Wisconsin, for Timmy Carver's funeral. It
didn't matter if she missed Jason's soccer game or ladies night.
She had to say goodbye to Timmy, even though she hadn't
seen him in twenty-three years.

Because Timmy, a decorated firefighter, had come home
safely after rushing to help out at Ground Zero, emerged from
long, angry blazes that had killed or maimed his friends, and
survived a relationship with Becca, she'd assumed he'd been
assigned some kind of guardian angel. He slipped in his bath-
tub, broke his neck, and died instantly, survived by his widow,
Elizabeth, and four children, or so the obituary read. She'd
been checking the *Rhinelander Daily News* online for tidbits
about Timmy ever since she discovered the great information
superhighway. Last night she found the obituary after logging
on to book a surprise trip to Israel for Adam's fiftieth birthday.

She zipped a toothbrush, toothpaste, floss, moisturizer, and comb into her toiletries bag, then decided she'd better try on the outfit, which she hadn't worn since her mother's funeral. After dropping her sweatpants and tank top in a heap, she paused to examine her reflection in the full-length bathroom mirror. Her breasts had kept enough shape that she could go braless without looking like a slattern, and her belly was borderline bikini-friendly, which was more than most mothers of two teenage boys could say. But who was she trying to impress anyway? Was Timmy going to wink at her from his open casket in acknowledgment of her ass, firmed by pole-dancing classes, if still a little bigger than she'd hoped?

The skirt and jacket fit her perfectly. Becca hung them on a wooden hanger, removed the dry-cleaning plastic from one of Adam's shirts, and slid it over the suit. Curls still damp, she went down to the kitchen wearing her nice jeans, a black V-neck sweater, and a necklace she'd made at a beading retreat. Adam had brewed her a pot of green tea. Sweet Adam. He'd never complained about covering carpools and meals when she spent weeknights studying for her bat mitzvah, or went off for five days to a yoga retreat at Kripalu, or attended a weeklong shamanic conference in Taos, returning home with a tattooed ankle.

Becca loved Adam with equal commitment. And she'd mothered hard: she'd pulverized carrots in the food processor when the boys were babies, managed Jason's soccer teams, and stalked the Washington area's coveted guitar teacher until he agreed to give Isaac private lessons.

She spread a piece of wheat toast with goat cheese and took

her plate and perfectly prepared cup of tea out to the porch. Thank God for Sudafed, though she'd gladly endure ragweed season in return for the gold and red leaves, rich with the scent of their sweet decay. A native Californian, she loved how the change of seasons held the possibility of things to come. After she finished her tea and locked up the house, she returned to the glider and waited for the cab.

She and Adam had been waiting for this cab for years.

─────────

Becca had wanted Timmy Carver to love her so much that he'd kill for her. She'd have settled for a smile during their five-hour drive to his parents' cabin up north, in the part of Wisconsin shaped like a thumb. They'd fought hard last night, and she wondered if this could be the argument that broke them.

Every forty miles or so, she reached over and snaked her index finger under his shorts and the new Bucky Badger boxers she'd given him for his birthday. He clenched his teeth so hard that she could see the little muscles moving around in his jaw, and fixed his blue eyes, round as poker chips, on the pine trees and black-eyed Susans that made her sneeze and wheeze. Lynyrd Skynyrd drowned out any prospect of conversation.

They passed two signs: one for a deer crossing, the other a square brown wooden one carved with a rendering of an American Indian in a feathered headdress under yellow block letters that read "Minocqua 5 Miles."

Becca broke the silence. "Let's stop. I have to go to the bathroom."

Timmy pulled into the driveway of the Minocqua Soda

and Fudge Shoppe. "I'll wait."

She glanced at his bowed head before she let herself out of the truck. He was still smarting from Becca's words. Last night she'd called him an emotional miser.

The store smelled like the pine-scented candles accenting the display of brightly beaded moccasins, leather wristbands, and Escape to Wisconsin T-shirts. A large blond woman wearing a suede vest and a name tag that read "Patty" smiled at Becca, and Becca bought a half pound of walnut fudge in exchange for Patty's kindness.

Timmy had rolled down the window, and he was flicking his Schlitz key chain back and forth against the dashboard in time with the music blaring from his stereo. She had a childish urge to walk past the truck, so he'd have to drive after her. She'd get hit by a car and he'd rush her to the hospital and donate his blood to keep her alive. Jesus, she was desperate. She slid into the passenger's seat and handed him the white box with the gold Minocqua Fudge sticker.

"Peace offering," she practically shouted. She moved so close to him that the blond fuzz on his thighs grazed her bare leg.

"I just don't know what you want from me, Becca." He accepted the box. "Should I rent the Goodyear Blimp and fly over Madison with a big sign that says 'I love Becca Coopersmith'?"

Beats the car accident idea.

He looked down at his lap. "I don't think I can give you what you need."

"Come on, Timmy. How hard would it have been for you to buy me a birthday card?" Her panic that he'd leave her crested into that familiar wave that washed over her.

He started to grind his teeth again.

One. Two. Three. Four. She buried her face in her hands. Five. Six. Seven. Breathe. Say something neutral. She'd turned into this sorry-ass girlfriend who groveled for scraps of love like her parents' dog, Hendrix. He died choking on a wishbone.

He opened the box and handed her a piece of fudge. "Let's have a nice time."

"I'm nervous." What if his parents saw how miserable she made their son?

"Just be yourself." Their equilibrium had been restored; Timmy was telling her what to do.

Be myself? Mouthy Jewish girl from the wrong side of Beverly Hills?

By the time they pulled up to Timmy's parents' cabin, they'd eaten the whole half pound of fudge and had fondled each other to the point of heated distraction. Both ravenous and carsick, Becca craved something substantial, like a steak or a hunk of cheese. It was still light out, because that's how it was at nine o'clock at night in northern Wisconsin in June.

Timmy's dad cupped a sweating can of Schlitz and gave his son a "Well, what have we here?" look. "You must be Becca. Damned glad to meet ya." He extended his hand.

"Nice to meet you too, Bud."

His father looked surprised.

Should she have called him Mr. Carver? "You look exactly like Timmy around the eyes," she said. He did.

Bud gazed off toward the lake in the same way that Timmy

did when she complimented him. Timmy's mother emerged from the cabin smoothing the waist of her culottes. A visor kept strands of her grayish-brown hair from falling into her eyes. Timmy and his parents were built like greyhounds.

Okay, no calling her Dot. "Nice to meet you, Mrs. Carver," Becca said, embracing her. Becca was from a family of big huggers. Mrs. Carver stepped back and patted her on the back formally. The brisk northern air had already chilled Becca, and she folded her arms over her chest.

Becca tried harder over dinner: potato salad, steaks on the grill, and iceberg lettuce. Who ate iceberg lettuce?

"So why the fascination with indigenous people up here?" she asked, spearing a mayonnaise-soaked potato, genuinely wanting to learn more about the North Woods.

Timmy and his parents looked at each other.

"Well, you're in Indian country," Bud said. "Menominee to be exact. Did you see the reservation—"

She cut him off mid-sentence. "Did you ever read that book? Can't remember the name. The one about fetal alcohol syndrome?" In her enthusiasm for the topic, Becca forgot to swallow fully before talking, and a white fleck of potato flew across her plate onto the green tablecloth.

Becca was used to expressing her opinions at the family dinner table. Her mother, a reading specialist, and her father, a hippie turned Beverly Hills High history teacher, would look at her with admiration, and then they'd bait her into an argument until everyone was screaming and yelling at each other at the top of their lungs. Finally someone would say something irreverent and wickedly funny, and they would all laugh, and that would be that. Bud and Dot were not likely to say anything remotely wicked or funny.

"Becca wants to be a social worker," Timmy explained with a trace of pride in his voice.

His unexpected display of approval melted Becca. He dug a serving spoon into a bowl of Jell-O embedded with all sorts of crap, topped off with a layer of cream cheese. "Anybody want the rest of this?"

"You go ahead, Timmy," his mother said, and they all nodded. "Finish it up."

After dinner, as she dried the dishes, Becca asked Dot about Timmy's sister's kids — Bud Jr., seven, and Kerry, three and a half. Dot asked Becca nothing about herself, which should have cued Becca to refrain from relaying how she and Timmy met.

"It was a year ago this weekend, actually. Timmy and I were both at the Klinc Bar."

Dot didn't look up from her dishes, but Becca could tell she wanted to hear more by the way she turned the water down and cocked her head.

"He'd fought a big fire that day, an accident in a chem lab at the U." Becca paused, remembering his hair, wet and neatly parted to the side, and the powder-blue shirt that showed off his reddish tan. Adrenaline oozed out of every pore of his body, sending a current through the whole bar. Everyone wanted to touch him; his buddies couldn't stop patting him on the back, and she thought she'd die if she didn't get close enough at least to smell him. Big hero.

"Oh, sure, Timmy's always been the type to lend a hand."

Dot scrubbed a stubborn glob of red Jell-O from a bowl.

Becca told her about how they started playing darts — and how later she tracked down his fire station and called him up. This was the point when someone who was fond of her and appreciated her chutzpah would say something like, "No way!" Dot raised her eyebrows but still didn't look at Becca directly. She would freak Dot out if she added that Hannah had said that Timmy had become her new religion.

"And here we are." Becca paused and waited for Dot to say something, maybe offer up the lore of how she had met Bud. But then again, Becca sensed that Dot didn't want the same outcome for Becca and Timmy. When the kitchen was spotless, they all convened in the living room. Becca took in the assortment of dead animals decorating the walls. Bud and Dot divided the newspaper — sports and business for Bud, lifestyle and coupons for Dot — and settled into their matching recliner chairs. Timmy motioned toward the two bedrooms at the back of the cabin.

"Long drive." He stretched and yawned. "We're going to hit the hay."

"Sleep well," Dot and Bud replied in unison, and returned to their papers. No kiss, no hug.

A rusting clawfoot tub dominated the guest bathroom, and the toilet refilled with water one molecule at a time after flushing. Low water pressure. The last thing Becca wanted was to create some kind of sewage situation; she could hold it in for another day. She washed up with a cracked bar of Dial soap and crawled into her single bed, pulling the starched white sheets around her chin and waiting for Dot and Bud to go to sleep so Timmy could come and finish what they'd started during their drive. Timmy tiptoed into her room and got into bed with her.

"Your parents are going to hear everything," she whispered as quietly as she could.

"No screaming tonight." He kissed her.

The realization that Bud and Dot knew exactly what they were doing kept her on the brink of letting go. Timmy was at his most expressive when he was making love to her, especially after they'd fought. He gave her this vague grin that opened up his face like some kind of flower. Hannah speculated that Becca provoked fights for the makeup sex. Hannah didn't like Timmy; actually, she said she didn't like Becca around him, that she was too careful and quiet and fake.

She gazed up at his moonlit face. He always kept his eyes closed when they made love. She studied the purplish veins spidering along his eyelids until he collapsed on top of her. She stroked his back, noting the contrast between the olive tone in her skin and the pink in his. He peeled himself from her body and lay next to her to catch his breath.

"You'd better go back to your room." She ran her hand up his pelvis.

He kissed her breast through her T-shirt and rolled out of bed, pulling up his boxers as he left, his sinewy nakedness casting a shadow along the wall.

Alone in bed, she hugged herself in a futile attempt to stave off the insanely cold northern Wisconsin night.

After breakfast, they joined Bud and Dot for a walk through a patch of woods behind the cabin to pick blackberries. Becca's nose ran like a hose. Timmy and his parents said nothing as they tweezed blackberries from the bushes, nothing as they'd eaten their pancakes earlier that morning, nothing, nothing, nothing. They didn't talk politics or joke around or talk with their mouths full of food. They didn't talk at all.

By mid-morning, the waistband of Becca's jean shorts strained against her abdomen, bloated from holding in two days' worth of waste; mosquitoes had feasted on her calves, and Bud had pulled a tick off her neck.

"Got a treat for you, Timmy," Bud announced after a lunch of olive-loaf sandwiches on white bread, with potato chips and lukewarm lemonade. "Hank Sawyer gave us a couple of passes to see the Minocqua Bats."

"Bats?" God, no.

"Not real bats, Becca. They're professional water skiers, and boy, can they fly."

"Like bats." Relieved, Becca picked an olive from the loaf.

"You bet." Bud smiled.

Did that mean that they got to leave the compound? That she'd have a night out with Timmy? That she might find nirvana in a public bathroom? A sense of hope buoyed her, and four hours later, Timmy drove Becca to Minocqua, home of walnut fudge and her new best friend Patty.

"So, how am I doing?" She tried to sound casual, ironic.

"Good," he grunted, squinting into the sun.

"Your mom hates me," she said, hoping he'd deny it.

"You don't have to try so hard."

"You think I'm trying too hard?" she answered too quickly.

"Can we just have a good time?"

"I'll try."

"Good."

"But not too hard."

He grinned. She loved to make him smile.

Becca found the ladies' room immediately, ignoring a woman checking out her pink shoes. The woman and Dot wore the kind of sandals she always thought were designated for people with foot problems. Dr. Somethings. She didn't care; she felt lighter, and happy to be alone with Timmy.

She'd never seen anything like the Minocqua Bats. They were all fit, broad-shouldered, Nordic-looking people who whizzed off ramps, bodies perched precariously over their sleek slalom skis, like Olympic jumpers, or real bats flying into the fresh Wisconsin air. Free.

"So why are they called bats and not robins or bluebirds?" Becca took a swig of beer.

"Bats are the only mammal in the world naturally capable of flight." Timmy was an Eagle Scout and he knew a lot about animals and hardware stores. He also explained how bats saw better at night than any other mammal.

Maybe so, but she still loathed those disease-laden flying rodents, a fact she would never divulge to him.

Timmy and Becca drank beer and ate slices of pepperoni pizza on a faded orange blanket that Bud and Dot had probably picnicked on a million times while marveling at the very same feats. Becca leaned her back against Timmy's chest and relaxed into the rhythm of his warm breath on her hair. She wondered if anybody had ever died doing one of these jumps, but she said nothing. Timmy told her that she worried too much about dying and injuries. Clearly, stories of pogroms and genocide hadn't sullied his emotional DNA.

They lay on the blanket until it got dark. She'd never seen the stars from so far north; she felt like she could reach up and touch them with her fingertips.

"There's the Big Dipper. People say it looks like a ladle, but I think it looks more like a wagon." He took her hand in his and pointed it toward the sky. "That's the handle."

"I see it." It did look more like a wagon. Timmy was one of the smartest people she knew. A World War II buff and an avid reader of biographies of obscure scientists, he beat her at Trivial Pursuit every time.

Becca caught a chill during the drive home, so she unbuckled her seat belt and slid next to Timmy. He stuck a Charlie Daniels Band tape in the deck and thumped his fingers on the steering wheel to some song about the devil going to Georgia. She hadn't even bothered bringing her music on the trip — Laura Nyro, the Fairport Convention, Rickie Lee Jones — folky stuff her parents liked, too. Wanting more of him before they got back to his parents' cabin, she put her tongue in his ear and tasted his saltiness.

"Cut it out, Becca," he said, but she could tell that he liked what she was doing.

She nibbled his neck, where he was super ticklish, and he laughed. She could feel his muscles contract against her ribs.

The skinny road wound through stands of tall pines and birches. It was as black as a tunnel, no streetlights or vapor lamps. A station wagon full of drunk kids whirled by them, honking the horn; a girl with an auburn ponytail hung her head out the window and screamed, "Go, Badgers!"

Timmy shrugged. "Badger Country."

"Man, they're sloshed," Becca said, and tickled Timmy's neck again.

As his stomach contracted with a fresh giggle, a deer darted across the road. Seconds later, their truck hit the animal with a loud thud and the screeching of brakes. Becca flew forward, her shoulder smashing into the vent on the dashboard.

"Jesus Christ," Timmy muttered. "You okay?"

Becca nodded as adrenaline coursed through her body; she felt numb. "I think so." Her shoulder was beginning to throb.

Timmy's eyes narrowed into slits, hyper-alert, wild and calm at the same time, a more concentrated version of the expression he'd worn the night they met, after he'd fought that newsworthy fire. He pulled the truck over to the side of the road and left the engine running while he ran to the spot where the deer lay splayed on the asphalt. The truck's tail-lights cast a dull glow on the animal as it struggled to move its legs. Thank God. He hadn't killed it.

A flash of Timmy's sweatshirt disappeared into the forest on the other side of the road. Part of her wanted to chase after him, part of her wanted to drag the deer from the highway, but most of her just froze. She wadded up some tissue paper from the Minocqua Soda and Fudge Shoppe and wiped blood from her shoulder.

She watched for Timmy through the back window, which made her shoulder hurt even more. She felt better when he popped out of the woods carrying a rock the size of a bowling ball, moving awkwardly yet with the certainty of a man who ran five miles a day to keep in shape. A man who would walk into a burning building. He leaned down, lowering his body over the deer's, as he had over hers so many times. Against the star-filled sky, she could only make out his silhouette as he stood and raised the boulder over his head. Then he brought it down, and sediment met bone. When he came back to the truck, his face revealed an expression she'd never seen, a mixture of kindness and regret. And love.

They drove home in silence, except for the noise of the deer carcass sliding around in the back of the truck. For once she was grateful for the quiet. He reached out to her, and she slid next to him so that their thighs touched. She could feel his body heat through her jeans, that current from the Klinc Bar. Now it scared her.

Back at the cabin, he sent her inside while he dealt with the carcass. Bud and Dot were asleep. Becca lay trembling in her cold bed. When he came in, she avoided his gaze as he pulled back the covers and stood over her. He smelled like blood and sour sweat. A wet warmth soaked her thighs and Dot's sun-dried sheets. He slowly licked the palm of his hand and placed it on one nipple, then the other, and slid his hand down her belly until she arched her back, her body begging him to touch her. Eventually, he did.

He tipped her chin up, and she could smell herself on his finger. When she finally looked at him, she noticed a line of blood streaking his cheekbone. She saw everything in his eyes: tenderness and cruelty. She pulled him into her, knowing that she'd be a different person when they finished making love, when they finished scraping and scratching at the outer edges of who they were, when they finished with each other for good.

Becca arrived at the airport well in time for her flight. The sky looked like blue glass, and the low roar of airplane engines made her heart race. She walked quickly to the check-in counter and waited in line behind a young businessman sharing the importance of his cell phone call with the crowd.

Finally, her turn. A pleasant-looking woman with a Wisconsin accent like Timmy's asked for her confirmation number and photo ID. Becca reached into her bag to pull out her wallet, which felt slimmer than usual. The plastic case holding her credit card and driver's license was gone. She didn't even bother tearing the bag apart, because she remembered that she'd left the case next to her computer last night when she bought one plane ticket to Rhinelander and four to Tel Aviv. "Don't forget to put your license back in your purse," she'd reminded herself aloud. But she had.

The agent looked at her sympathetically. "You've got time," she said, glancing at Becca's wedding ring. "Can your husband bring you your license?"

"I don't think so," Becca answered.

Becca bought herself a bottled water and a slab of fudge from an airport candy stand and settled into a comfortable seat facing the window. She hadn't eaten fudge since her trip to Minocqua. She'd meditated, written dozens of bad poems, and even tried to find God in order to return to that place, a place inhabited by dead deer and pine trees and a decent man who would have destroyed her, brutally and without malice.

Perhaps she watched ten or fifteen planes take off; she lost count. At noon, she hailed a cab and went home. She put a frozen Tupperware container of veggie chili into the fridge for dinner, emptied the dishwasher, and returned her toiletries to their shelves and holders. She tore the plastic from her black suit and hung it next to Adam's naked shirt, so close that the garments touched.

MORE SO

Adam Kornfeld, July 2007

P*lease call Georgia Dumfries.* Adam glanced at the two-day-old message his assistant had scrawled on a Post-it note. He'd forgotten to return Georgia's call, confirmation that his one indiscretion in eighteen years of marriage hadn't affected him after all. He'd assumed that if he ever cheated on Becca he'd feel guilt or remorse or some kind of emotion that would surprise him entirely and erode his marriage. He loved his wife — even more so now — yet he would feel perfectly comfortable sharing an elevator with the woman he'd slept with on an innocuous Sunday evening last April while Becca and the boys circled Ben Gurion International Airport. A client emergency had kept him from enjoying his fiftieth birthday trip that Becca had organized.

He stared at his computer screen and thought about the night he'd bumped into Georgia at a trendy Woodley Park café. The month before, he'd hired her to edit an AFL-CIO video, and he figured he owed her a drink after trapping her in a windowless room with his OCD client for days on end. They drank too much red wine, shared an order of buffalo wings, and whispered in the gardens of the National Cathedral, two blocks from Georgia's apartment, their final destination for the evening. Adam made it home in time to watch the eleven o'clock news, one hour before he officially turned fifty. And one week after that, when Becca returned from Israel, tanned and spiritually sated, with an olive-wood sculpture for his office and a Ziploc baggie full of new pebbles for their fire pit, they skipped the season premiere of *The Sopranos* to make love in the shower.

He'd return Georgia's call on Tuesday, after the long Fourth of July holiday. He stacked papers in piles as he anticipated the weekend with Becca, the honeymoon period before the house would start sounding too quiet and they would surreptitiously glance at the calendar, eager for the boys to come home from summer camp. Tonight they would make love and then drift into a seamless sleep, without the worry that Isaac would have a car accident, without Jason's running cell phone patter with various members of the freshman class of Bethesda–Chevy Chase High. Becca would spend Saturday with her friend Hannah at some drum circle up in Baltimore while Adam slept late, futzed around on his guitar, and thumbed through the stack of *New Yorkers* that had accumulated next to his bed. They would enjoy a nice dinner — maybe Indian, the boys hated curry — and he'd convince her to catch the new Bruce Willis thriller with him.

Through a lazy smile, he crunched on a sliver of ice he'd mined from his morning iced Americano. His direct line rang. Must be Becca. "Kornfeld Group," he answered.

"Adam. It's Georgia."

He felt a surge of excitement at the sound of her voice and indulged himself with the image of her straddling him, blouse unbuttoned, lacy maroon bra exposed. "Georgia, hello!" he said with a bit too much enthusiasm.

The rest of the conversation was a blur, save for a string of words that stuck out like rusty nails through an old board. Ex-boyfriend. Gonorrhea. Before you put the condom on. Asymptomatic. Tested positive. So sorry. He ended the call quickly, and after he hung up, he put his clammy fingers to his temples, hot and pulsing. His heart crawled into his throat as he tried to remember how many times he'd thrust into Georgia before she diplomatically dislodged herself to retrieve a condom from her nightstand. Two? Three? Did it matter?

He Googled gonorrhea first, and then internists who practiced in Virginia. South of Fairfax County. A world away from his suburban Maryland home. He wasn't going to call David, his doctor and fellow member of the search committee for a new chief rabbi at their temple. Nobody could see him until Tuesday morning, 9:45 at the earliest. Ninety more hours. Ninety hours ago would have been Monday evening; he was talking to a social worker named Rhoda about when and where to move his mother. Alzheimer's.

He emailed Becca, knowing that he couldn't trust himself to talk to her: *New client called. Have to put together a dog and pony show for Tuesday. See you at 7. Love, A.*

He had to pee. He used a stall even though he was the only person left in the building. Everything felt like it should, a painless stream of coffee-scented urine. Then he sat on the toilet and inspected himself, the backs of his sweaty thighs sticking to the seat. No redness. No swelling. No gleet. Gleet. It was the kind of word Becca would serve up during a game of Scrabble; she'd reach for her worn *Oxford American Dictionary* and recite, "Gleet. Noun. The thick, copious urethral pus discharge associated with sexually transmitted diseases." She'd fold her lovely arms over her breasts, smug about her verbal acuity and presumed immunity from firsthand exposure to such a noun. And why not? What middle-aged former soccer coach, advocate for all the proper lefty causes, and master of the chords to every Crosby, Stills & Nash song ever written would infect his wife with the clap? Jesus.

His breathing felt shallow, and he wondered if he was having a heart attack, if he might die. His first impulse was not to call 911 or try out some of Becca's yoga breathing, but to go back online and tidy up his browser, removing the list of sites with the word "gonorrhea" attached to them.

His house looked different when he turned into the driveway. He took it in as if the bank might foreclose on it at any second: the big oak tree that hovered over the roof, scaring the crap out of Becca when the winds blew strong; Becca's blue-turned-purple hydrangeas encircling the front porch; the basketball hoop he'd won at the school raffle last fall; the squeaky swing where he'd spied Jason making out with his girlfriend, trying to cop a feel, and the fire pit out back.

The house smelled like challah and the chicken Becca was roasting. She had set the table for Shabbat. Odd. Normally the boys' absence meant Chinese takeout or omelets, "a Shabbat from Shabbat," Becca called it.

"I'm up here, babe," she hollered down from their bedroom.

The cicadas chirred so loudly he could hear them through the closed window; tonight the sound chafed his nerves. He poured himself a shot of vodka.

Becca appeared and kissed him on the mouth. "That new client driving you to drink already?"

He wasn't a very good liar, so he dodged the question. "Shabbat shalom?" He pointed to the candles with a questioning look.

"I was in the mood." She winked.

"Glad to hear it." He delivered the expected response and halfheartedly patted her ass.

Adam dimmed the lights, and Becca stood in front of the candlesticks, a wedding present from his sister, the blue and white ceramic slightly chipped. He'd never noticed that before. Becca ushered in the Sabbath with circular arm motions that culminated in covering her eyes. She always let her hands linger there for a minute to pray away her fears and take stock of all that was good — "blessing the hell out of life," she called it. She sang the prayer over the candles; as usual, it sounded like a Joni Mitchell song, pre-*Court and Spark*.

If the boys were here, Adam would feign disapproval while they teased Becca about her weekly Joni impersonation. But tonight the sound of her chanting — earnest, soulful, and a bit off key — impaled him. He'd heard her sing for the first time almost thirty years ago, when the staff of Camp Kehilah celebrated Shabbat two days before the campers arrived for the first session. Now the soft candlelight framed her curls, strands of gray flecking a shade of red that meant the hair would lose the rest of its pigment soon. Fine lines fanned out from the corners of her small blue eyes. Still, she didn't look much different from that fast-talking BU freshman he'd fallen in love with at first sight.

It occurred to him then that Becca was built like — well, Georgia. Same small breasts and waist, same round hips and wiry hair. But Georgia, a quiet observer, would never have helped him lead a dining hall packed with a hundred and seventy-five kids in a light-bulb-rattling rendition of "Dodi Li," or enrolled in a pole-dancing class to shake her middle-aged booty with abandon.

"Earth to Adam." Becca interrupted his thoughts. "You going to do the kiddush?"

He could detect the tightness in his voice as he raced through the blessing over the wine. In two weeks' time, when the boys returned home from camp, would he place his hands over their heads and murmur the blessings, or would his family have been decimated by his reckless stupidity?

Sitting across from Becca, chewing her fresh-baked challah, he could barely taste what might be the last Shabbat meal as he knew it. He half listened as Becca described her road trip to Baltimore with Hannah the next morning for a women's drum circle she'd talked Hannah into trying. Becca had embraced the Landmark Forum, veganism, and the La Leche movement with passion. She'd studied the Torah with their rabbi to prepare for her adult bat mitzvah ceremony the year she turned forty-five. She'd filled notebooks with bad poetry and trotted off to exotic locales to attend writing seminars that only confirmed her lack of talent. She didn't care; she loved the energy.

Thank God for Becca's new hot yoga class; she'd fallen asleep with her reading glasses perched on the end of her nose and a copy of *The Audacity of Hope* splayed across a sexy black camisole. She'd worn a skirt with no panties to dinner, and he knew she meant business; he'd have had to feign some horrible ailment to spurn her overtures. His bones ached from the exhaustion of living with his secret. Eighty-three more hours and he'd find out what he'd done. Eighty-three hours ago would have been Tuesday morning. He'd just given his office manager, Lizzie, a month off to help out with her grandchildren in Arizona. Her son had electrocuted himself to death last month.

He peeled down to his boxers, swallowed a couple of Dramamine, and waited for the usual wave of drowsiness to engulf him. He dreamt about a bat. He and Becca used to sneak off to an empty cabin at Camp Kehilah to make love. One night they fell asleep and woke at dawn to find a bat perched on the torn blue-and-white-striped mattress. Eleven months later, a hysterical Becca called his college dorm to tell him she'd read that bats' teeth are so small that they can bite people without their feeling it, that bats are the most rabid animals in the world, that she and Adam should have their spinal fluid tested for exposure, that rabies makes you die a neurological nightmare of a death. If they experienced no symptoms after a year, they'd be safe. For the next month, he called twice a day, subsidizing his phone bill by bartending at a small tavern just north of campus.

Adam awoke from his batmare at 3:15 a.m. Gonorrhea aside, he couldn't shake a vague feeling of dread, as if he'd been bitten by something rabid long before he slept with Georgia.

Becca's alarm sounded at the crack of dawn. She fumbled around for her yoga clothes, and when she kissed Adam goodbye, he could smell her body lotion and a hint of garlic from last night's chicken. The thought of Georgia jumped out at him the way Jason used to when they were playing hide-and-seek. He'd first met her at a barbecue hosted by his neighbors Tad and Nikki, when he accidentally squirted ketchup on her white tank top; she laughed, and her breath smelled clean, like seltzer water or air.

Adam tossed and turned for hours, trying to go back to sleep. He hadn't stayed in bed this long since Isaac brought home the rotavirus from preschool, and then a lot of throwing up was involved. This morning he felt like that big oak tree in the front yard had landed on his chest. He didn't move, except to pee twice. Still no burning or any other signs. A raging caffeine headache roused him from his bed at one in the afternoon.

He took his coffee up to the attic and began looking through old photographs. He pulled out an album his mother had given him before she started losing her memory: 1960, Adam wearing a pointy hat and blowing out three birthday candles; 1970, Adam becoming a bar mitzvah; 1974, Adam practicing a 1-4-5 chord pattern on his cousin's Gibson.

A loose wedding photo fell out of the album: Becca grinning, wearing a flowered wreath around her head and a long veil that came down to her ankles. He found another photo taken under the chuppah: Adam standing between Becca and his mother, whose pink suit hung on her formerly plump body. She'd lost fifteen pounds since the fitting, the day before Adam's father turned fifty. The day he died.

Adam pulled out Becca's old summer camp album and pored over photos of the two of them posing with their favorite campers. Becca wore a brown two-piece bathing suit and friendship bracelets up and down her forearms and in clusters around her ankles. The kids idolized her, and every guy at camp wanted a piece of her. He'd felt lucky that she was his.

The last two pages of the album were filled with photos of Becca and the fireman who broke her heart. Timmy Carver. Her grand love, borderline obsession. Adam once overheard Becca announce to her book club that she'd married him because he fit like an old pair of Birkenstocks, but that Timmy was the one that got away. How absurd — Becca boiling bratwursts and guzzling beer with the firefighters of Minocqua, Wisconsin. Who the hell lives in Wisconsin?

An old fury grabbed hold of him. He shoved the albums into the cobwebs and went downstairs to make banana pancakes, leaving a big puddle of batter on the counter; he'd feast on his Timmy Carver anger like a German shepherd on a porterhouse. Becca's words swirled around in his head. An old pair of Birkenstocks. The guy with the guitar, every summer camp has one, an NJB, a nice Jewish boy. Well, maybe this NJB wasn't so N after all. The phone rang.

"Dad, it's me," Jason said in his man-boy voice.

Adam practically jumped through the phone line. "Hey, big guy! How's it going up there?"

"I slalomed today." Jason's excitement bubbled under his matter-of-fact delivery of the news.

Adam imagined the camp's lethargic motorboat pulling skinny Jason as he squinted into the Maine sun, his nose red and peeling. "Way to go, J."

"Where's Mom?"

"Up in Baltimore," Adam said, playing the abandoned husband. Ridiculous. He'd wanted her to go, not to mention the fact that he might have given her VD. "With Hannah."

Jason handed the phone over to Isaac, newly smitten with some seventeen-year- old sailing instructor. Isaac reminded Adam of himself, the guy with the guitar and minimal athletic ability.

"Listen, steer clear of bats," Adam warned Isaac impulsively. Isaac laughed. "You sound like Mom."

"Do I?" Adam could picture Isaac shaking his head, pony-tail bouncing back and forth over his shoulder.

"You've never heard her give the bat lecture?" Isaac raised his voice an octave. "You see one of those flying rodents, boys, and you run like a bat out of hell. One bite can ruin your life, and you won't even know it until it's too late."

Adam could just see Becca waving her finger at the boys. "Now I've been properly bat-tized."

"That's just wrong, Dad." Isaac chuckled. "So wrong."

The Timmy Carver anger hadn't even lasted through the phone call; Adam couldn't touch his stack of pancakes. Becca was the love of his life, even if he wasn't hers. Besides, Timmy died last fall. He glanced at the clock. Seventy-two more hours. Seventy-two hours ago, he was standing in line at the Greek deli on 20th and M, perusing the *City Paper*, debating whether to splurge on the gyros or have the salad. Dressing on the side. He wasn't fat, but the week before, his doctor had given him a stern talking-to about his cholesterol, in view of what had happened to his dad. He went with the gyros, double order of lamb.

He thought about contacting Georgia, because he'd been a jerk to her. After lecturing Isaac and Jason ad nauseam about safe sex, how could he have been so stupid? He should apologize. Sorry, Georgia, for practically hanging up on you when you called to tell me that I might have ruined my life. Sorry, Georgia, for assuming that you'd been waiting patiently for some arrogant fuck to grant you a quickie. Sorry, Georgia, for bolting out the door before I'd even buckled my pants.

Georgia. Funny woman to select for a fling. She wasn't younger or prettier or smarter than Becca. She wasn't desperate, but he had a sense that unlike Becca she'd be happy with whatever he could give her, a kiss, a night, or a slim offering of remorse after acting like a jerk. Becca was never satisfied. She picked through every peach at the grocery store to make sure she selected the best one. She'd renovated their kitchen twice, hectored principals to make sure that the boys got the best teachers, and switched exercise regimens every six months to challenge her metabolism. Women both envied and snickered at her, and men lit up around her, especially when she pranced around in her sexy Catwoman costume at the neighborhood Halloween parties.

He spent the next four hours flipping between infomercials, a fly-fishing show, and an old Court TV documentary about the Menendez brothers. He drank tumblers of ice water so he could revel in the small consolation that he was still pissing without pain. At five, he showered. He scrubbed his thighs, up to his groin, harder and harder until his skin turned raw. The physical pain was a relief. He squirted a blob of Becca's shampoo on his hand, closed his eyes, and inflicted the same scrubbing on his head; cutting into his bald spot with his fingernails.

"Hey." Becca materialized, water streaming down her shoulders.

He recoiled. "You scared the holy fuck out of me, Becca." He jumped out of the shower and wrapped himself in a towel. "What were you thinking?"

Becca stood there under the spray looking like a little girl whose brand-new dress had just been splattered with mud by the playground bully. She turned off the water and dried herself off.

He wanted to grab her so badly, but her nakedness scared him. He was afraid to touch her. Despite his squeaky-clean skin, he'd never felt so filthy. "I'm sorry, I'm just out of sorts."

Becca still looked hurt and confused. "What's up?" She moved to hug him.

He backed away. "Work stuff," he grumbled.

"The schmucks who kept you from your fiftieth birthday

trip to Israel?" Becca switched moods deftly, angry now. "You just tell them that you'll have to charge them double if they're going to be unreasonable." Any enemy of Adam's was an enemy of hers.

Becca wasn't a great listener; she was too quick to offer a solution or an opinion, which annoyed him. But he was in no position to be annoyed. "I guess I shouldn't let them get to me."

She ran her hand down his back. "Let's go out."

They snuck tomato, mozzarella, and basil sandwiches into an art theater and endured a movie about a skinny Japanese businessman who fucks his cheeky Australian tour guide somewhere in the outback and then dies. Agitating as hell. Not that Adam could have concentrated on that new Bruce Willis movie anyway. He took Becca's hand, and after a few minutes she leaned over to whisper, "A little lighter, babe. I can feel my bones kissing."

They walked through Chinatown, now McBarnes and Nobled out. Depressing. They didn't talk until they were facing each other over cups of Häagen-Dazs, licking Rum Raisin and Java Chip off their respective spoons.

"Tell me about Baltimore," Adam said.

Becca grinned, flashing one of her dimples. "You'll glaze over if I start describing chants and homemade drums."

True. "How's Hannah?"

"Crazy nuts planning Goldie's bat mitzvah."

Adam could tell that Becca was about to launch into one of her speeches about how smart and lucky and spiritually grounded they were to have bar mitzvahed Isaac and Jason in Israel, avoiding the *Goodbye, Columbus* syndrome. He headed her off with a report on Jason's new waterskiing feat and Isaac's recitation of Becca's bat-out-of-hell warning.

"Do they know about that?" Adam bit down on a piece of Heath bar.

"You mean our rabies scare?" Becca laughed.

"I can't believe you dumped me after that." The petulance in his voice served as his tired ploy to make her proclaim her love for him, to swab an old wound. He was an asshole to ask for this.

Becca looked flattered. "You won in the end." She could barely suppress a smile.

"I was the consolation prize," he moped.

"Are we really talking about this?" Becca dabbed her mouth with a napkin.

He swirled his spoon around his ice cream cup. "I was there for you when you were freaking out about the bat, and then you took off with Mr. Aryan of the Great White North."

"Oh, God. It had nothing to do with the bat!" She did smile now, a little patronizingly. "On second thought, it had everything to do with the bat. You were so incredibly sweet and loving, and that scared me more than the rabies."

"What scared you?"

"That at nineteen I'd met the man I was going marry." She touched her pinkie to his cheek with such tenderness it gave him chills.

So the bat had cemented their relationship by scaring her off? Adam's head hurt. "Maybe we could have had this conversation thirty years ago."

"It wouldn't have changed anything." She wiped a glob of chocolate from his chin and licked her finger, her eyes warm. "We're here, aren't we?"

"You're right." Sitting across from Becca, he felt the way he had when his father bought him a guitar they couldn't afford. Her unfailing belief in their marriage, normally something he drew strength from, made him feel even punier. He turned away and tossed his ice cream dish and spoon into the trash can behind him.

They drove home in silence. Adam spent the balance of the evening drinking water, peeing, and checking himself. He called his mother, and when she confused him for his father, he hung up. Becca made four attempts to beckon him to their bed before she gave up. He fell asleep on the couch with his clothes on so that his morning hard-on would be safe from Becca's hands.

He awoke late. Becca was already downstairs. He tuned his guitar, but couldn't muster up the energy or the attention to play anything. Becca went for a long walk, thumbed through the *Post*, and fixed them a bowl of tuna salad, which they scooped up with long rectangular crackers sprinkled with all sorts of seeds. Adam couldn't bring himself to tell her that a caraway had lodged between her front two teeth.

He couldn't breathe. "I'm going to the office." He rose and kissed the top of her head.

"Oh, babe. Well, if you have to. But don't forget, we're

meeting Hannah, Danny, Maggie, and Eric for the fireworks at seven. It's a Solonsky night. No Amy and Leon, though, too late for the baby. Who would have thunk?" she prattled on as he headed for the door.

Adam sat in his steamy Subaru for a second before he started it. The heat offered him a welcome distraction. After a few minutes, he turned on the ignition. The clock read 12:45. Forty-five more hours until he'd know. Forty-five hours ago, Georgia had called him. If he hadn't spilled ketchup on her at that party, he never would have thought to hire her. If he'd had the balls to tell his client that their video could wait until after his birthday trip to Israel, he would have been circling Ben Gurion airport with his family that night last April. If he hadn't had a bad chimichanga once at the Mexican restaurant where he'd parked his car, he would have eaten there and not at the trendy bistro half a block away where he'd bumped into Georgia. Dayenu. History in the subjunctive. A term he'd heard in a movie once.

He thought back to the boys' childhood, when Jason could never resist the urge to smash Isaac's elaborate Lego constructions. Becca blamed it on sibling rivalry, but Adam understood the impulse to destroy something beautiful. To soil his marriage with a night he barely remembered beyond a maroon bra. Now he knew that he'd been afraid. Afraid to turn fifty. Afraid that if he didn't knock over his near-perfect Lego life, God would destroy it on His terms. Slowly, as with Adam's mother, who'd put a brand-new pair of heels in the freezer and a melting carton of ice cream in her shoe rack. Suddenly, as with his dad, whose arteries blew out while he was brunching at the twenty-dollar-a-head Palm Springs restaurant he couldn't afford. Explosively, as with his assistant's son, who suffered one unlucky jolt while trying to fix his air-conditioning unit on a 110-degree desert afternoon.

Adam fiddled with the vents so that air blew on his perspiring face. He put the gear shift in reverse and backed out of the driveway. As he pulled away from his house, he glanced in the rearview mirror long enough to spot Becca standing in front of her faded hydrangeas, her hands hidden in the pockets of thirty-year-old overalls stained with fresh dirt and the orange paint they'd used to fix up the Camp Kehilah counselors' lounge the summer they met. Her curls were tucked into a straw hat she'd begun wearing only recently, after her skin started sprouting big brown spots. She waved, or maybe readjusted her hat; he couldn't tell for sure.

The July sun, naked and bold, cast a luscious haze on the pink and red crape myrtles that lined Bertrand Court. He drove to the end of the block, past Marcus and Robin's house, where Isaac had dislocated his shoulder on the trampoline; past Tad and Nikki's front lawn, where Danny had recently installed an "Under Contract" sign; and past Maggie and Eric's driveway, where Amy and Leon were unbuckling Simon from his car seat. He turned out of the neighborhood and drove on, passing the pharmacy that filled his Lipitor prescription and the little Italian place where he picked up dinner when Becca didn't feel like cooking. He rolled down the window, inviting the hot sunshine onto his freckled skin, and waved his arms in circles, ushering in every memory and dream, blessing the hell out of life.

ACKNOWLEDGMENTS

Thank you to the editors of *Lilith Magazine, the minnesota review, Fifth Wednesday Journal*, PoliticsDaily.com, *Electric Grace: Still More Fiction by Washington Area Women, Blackbird, The Pedestal Magazine, Drash, Potomac Review, River Oak Review, Jewish Women's Literary Annual, Literary Mama, Shortbread Stories*, and *Bethesda Magazine*, where earlier versions of these stories first appeared; to the editors of *Shebooks* for publishing "Sylvia's Spoon" and "Shhh" as an ebook entitled *We Named Them All*; to the editors of the *Pushcart Prize Anthology* for the selection of "More So" as an honorable mention; to Pati Griffith for awarding "Harvard Man" the F. Scott Fitzgerald Prize; to Yona Zeldis McDonough for choosing "Sylvia's Spoon" for the *Lilith Magazine* Fiction Award; and to Mark Farrington and David Everett for their belief and for nominating "Shhh" for inclusion in *The Best New American Voices*.

I am the luckiest writer on the planet to be a member of a dream team that includes Prospect Park Books and the tireless and smart Jill Marr of the Sandra Dijkstra Literary Agency. I owe a debt of gratitude to Patty O'Sullivan (and Jill again) for plucking my debut novel, *Washing the Dead*, from the slush pile and thus launching my publishing journey, and to Colleen Dunn Bates for her editing and marketing genius, grace, and infectious enthusiasm for all things literary.

I wrote *Bertrand Court* over a span of fifteen years, so it would be impossible for me to acknowledge every reader who has helped me shape this material and in turn my narrative voice. Most of them, however, belong to one or more of the following communities to which I am forever indebted: The Writer's Center, the Johns Hopkins MA in Writing Program, the Glen Echo writing group, the George Washington University Creative Writing program, the DCJCC Writers Group, and the DC Women Writers. I'd also like to acknowledge my MacArthur Boulevard walking buddies and former Adas Israel Chavurah. Special thanks to Joy Johannessen for shining up my prose and helping me stitch these stories together.

With deepest gratitude, I'd like to acknowledge my mentors and muses: Faye Moskowitz, Bob Bausch, Margaret Meyers, Ed Perlman, Richard Peabody, Bill Loizeaux, and, specifically, Ray "Bertrand" Farkas, for teaching me how to eavesdrop properly and see life through the luscious haze of a pro-mist filter. I am grateful to my children, Gabriela and Gideon, for redefining my notion of love, which they do every single day; my parents, Lotta and Stuart Brafman, for providing encouragement and a quiet place to write; and my husband, Tom Helf, for his formidable PR efforts and, more importantly, for reading me on and off the page with honesty and great tenderness.

Michelle Brafman is the author of *Washing the Dead*. Her short fiction and essays have appeared in *The Washington Post, Tablet,* the *Los Angeles Review of Books, Slate, Lilith Magazine, the minnesota review,* and elsewhere. She teaches fiction writing at the Johns Hopkins University MA in Writing Program and lives in Glen Echo, Maryland, with her husband and two children.